Praise for the
## MUSIC OF THE HEART Series

"*The Longing Season* brings to life the reason for hymns—the ache of longings and struggles before we can sing of acceptance and joy. This hymn series provides wonderful, true-to-life insights that have me saying, 'I can relate to that.' Excellent writing and inspiring reading."

—**Marsha Blackburn**, Member of Congress

"Christine Schaub has written an excellent book filled with memorable characters, both historical and fictional, and truly capturing the essence of the time period about which she writes. *Finding Anna* is a real page-turner, a novel that both entertains the mind and inspires the imagination. Four stars!"

—**Craig Hart**, *CraigHart.net*

"Schaub's debut in the MUSIC OF THE HEART series deserves a standing ovation. She has given flesh to historical figures and illuminated redemptive suffering."★★★★½ FANTASTIC-Keeper

–*Romantic Times*

"*Finding Anna* is a superbly written and researched story, based on the lives of historical figures. I look forward to additional volumes in the MUSIC OF THE HEART series."

—**Melissa Parcel**, *Bookloons.com*

"A book of tragedy and hope, Schaub's *Finding Anna* is well worth the read. It quietly ignites in the reader a spark of thankfulness and a growing confidence of God's deep peace revealed in the midst of unspeakable heartache."

—**Kay Tira**, *Author's Choice Reviews*

"*Finding Anna* is a terrific inspirational historical biographical novel. . . . Readers will cherich the first MUSIC OF THE HEART tale and look forward to more such stories behind the hymns."

—**Harriet Klausner**, *ReviewCentre.com*

"I have to admit, I was hooked from the start!"

—**Deb Porter**, editor, *FaithWriters' Magazine*

"As a Jewish non-Christian, I found the book quite enjoyable as a story about that period. It's great historical fiction that happens to have a Christian message/theme. Good history, not just good Christian history. Very readable history!"

—**Barbara Cohen**, Irvington Writer's

"Christine Schaub breathes compelling life into this story—the first in her new and innovative MUSIC OF THE HEART series. The story is gripping and the development of characters and their situations is effective and shows a deft hand. This is a must-read for people who love inspirational historical romances!"
    —**Audrey Lawrence**, The Romance Studio

"I eagerly anticipate reading future novels in this interesting series. Hats off to Ms. Schaub for an excellent and well-written behind-the-scenes novel sure to be on many keeper shelves."
    —**Sherri Myers**, *romancejunkies.com*

"This was a deeply religious book, themed primarily around the prodigal son story, and is full of the example of two people who faced heartrending tragedy with a view to always help others, despite their limitations. *Finding Anna* can be enjoyed as a good novel, but [it] intends to be more than just entertainment."
    —**Heather Hiestand**, *Romance Readers at Heart*

"This was an amazing story! Ms. Schaub is off to a great start with her new series, and this is one read that I highly recommend. This is a read that will make you think, but at the same time entertain. This is truly a read that will touch your emotions."
    —**Inspirational Romance Writers**

"*Finding Anna* wraps a beautiful story around one of our most beloved hymns. It provides readers the opportunity to become aware of the depth of worldly sorrow that enveloped the hymn's writer, and the faith and hope that allowed him to proclaim, 'It is well with my soul.'"
    —**Marsha Blackburn**, Member of Congress

"This was an extrordinary read. This author's unique voice, well-written and fast-paced read was a joy making me both laugh and cry. If good things come in small packages, then you are in for a real treat with this . . . very powerful and poignant story found in Christine Schaub's *The Longing Season*—the second book in her MUSIC OF THE HEART series."
    —**Marilyn Rondeau**, Reviewer's International Organization (RIO)

# THE
# LONGING
# SEASON

Christine Schaub

MUSIC OF THE HEART

BETHANYHOUSE

MINNEAPOLIS, MINNESOTA

*The Longing Season*
Copyright © 2006
Christine Schaub

Cover design by Lookout Design Group, Inc.

Published by Bethany House Publishers
11400 Hampshire Avenue South
Bloomington, Minnesota 55438

Bethany House Publishers is a division of
Baker Publishing Group, Grand Rapids, Michigan.

Printed in the United States of America

ISBN-13:   978-0-7642-0060-1
ISBN-10:   0-7642-0060-7

**Library of Congress Cataloging-in-Publication Data**

Schaub, Christine.
    The longing season / Christine Schaub.
        p.   cm. — (Music of the heart)
        ISBN 0-7642-0060-7 (pbk.)
    1. Newton, John, 1725-1807—Fiction.  2. Hymns—Authorship—Fiction.
3. Hymn writers—Fiction.  4. Musical fiction.  I. Title.  II. Series: Schaub, Christine.
Music of the heart.
    PS3619.C333L66    2006
    813'.6—dc22                          2006013583

For my parents,
Raymond and Sondra Schaub,
who met my endless creative adventures with
"If it doesn't work out, you can always come home."
I love you for that.

# FROM THE AUTHOR

C hances are good that if you're reading the MUSIC OF THE HEART series, you're already a hymn lover. Like me, you might be at any church-oriented event, hear a brief refrain, and your heart goes, "Ohh . . . I love that hymn."

Why do our hearts do that? I have a theory.

When we first learned the hymn—usually as a child in church—we were sophisticated enough to recognize that the words of a meaningful poem married the notes of a memorable tune. As both we and the hymn matured, the music remained the same, but the words took on different and deeper meanings. And this is why I focus on the story behind the words.

While researching hymns, I found it interesting that those written for the early established church were composed for three similar meters. This was because hymns were *chanted*—they were poetry readings en masse. Think of the rich plainsong melody behind "Of the Father's Love Begotten." It was Martin Luther, that great challenger of the church, who bucked the system and set the words to established folk tunes.

Congregants responded by singing loudly and lustily, belting out the words they'd previously mumbled, memorizing long poems of praise, adoration, or contemplation. Suddenly, they *liked* singing the hymns. And so it was, and continues to be, a successful marriage.

I hope, as you continue to read this series, you'll find your-self more engaged in the hymn-singing process. I hope you'll take a closer look at that page in the hymnal, note the poet's name at the left and the composer's on the right, and wonder, as I do—*What's the story behind this one?*

## Time Is

*Too Slow for those who Wait,*
*Too Swift for those who Fear,*
*Too Long for those who Grieve,*
*Too Short for those who Rejoice;*
*But for those who Love,*
*Time is not.*

— Henry Van Dyke

# PROLOGUE

*Olney, England*
*December 31, 1772*

T he vicar stood at the frosty window of the attic room squinting out at the snow, contemplating his next move.

In his right hand he cradled the clay bowl of his favorite Alderman, the tobacco glowing red in the window's reflection as he rhythmically drew air through the long stem. His left hand held a soft leather-bound book that he tapped against his leg as he stared out at nothing, deep in conflicted thought.

He'd found the book exactly where he'd known it would be—in the desk's bottom drawer, hidden under a secret compartment. There were two others like it in that drawer, each one written in a careful hand, each page full of names, dates, and observations that were both revealing and . . . disturbing. The carefully—or carelessly—recorded information could answer age-old questions, entertain with peculiar detail, or crush with significance.

He understood the intrigue of a book like this left behind for curious eyes. And that was what he contemplated as he puffed and tapped . . . puffed and tapped.

He suddenly pivoted on his heel and marched over to the

grate. The fire both warned and beckoned him, and he thrust the book over the flames, intending to drop it in . . . but the dancing light illumined the wall directly above him. He looked up, hand still outstretched, and read the words painted there:

> " Thou shalt remember that thou wast
> a bond-man in the land of Egypt,
> and the Lord thy God redeemed thee."
>
> — Deu. XV. 15th.

He closed his eyes, clutched the book to his chest, and rested his forehead on the mantelpiece. *Thou shalt remember* . . . All manner of images—lurid and beautiful—tore through his mind. Even after all this time, his memory would not separate the wheat from the chaff.

He was sweating from the fire and the anxiety of the moment, his pulse pounding in his ears. He backed away and shook his head. Impulsiveness still plagued him after two decades of discipline. He feared he would never overcome it.

A great leather chair sat before the fire, and he settled the book on its arm, running his fingers over the worn cover. *Thou shalt remember* . . . He sighed.

His pipe had grown cold. He selected a piece of kindling from the copper basket on the hearth, fired the tip, and relit the tobacco in his Alderman. Then he took a seat in the great chair, placed the book on his lap, laid back his head . . . and remembered.

# PART I

*I am fond of them,*
    *of the inferior beings of the abyss,*
*of those who are full of longing.*

    —RICHARD WAGNER

# CHAPTER

## 1

*Plantain Island, Sierra Leone*
*January 1746*
*Twenty-six years earlier . . .*

N ewton lay where he'd collapsed, his trembling hands clutching the rope, his cheek against the smooth wood.

In his mind's eye he saw them there—the Marines with their muskets, the officers in full-dress uniform with their swords. Through the roaring in his ears, he heard the six bells signaling the forenoon watch and the call for all hands to witness punishment.

The master-at-arms brought the charge of desertion against him, and Newton nearly choked on his rage. Desertion! He had no more deserted than enlisted! He'd simply left to find his father. If any man could gain his release from Navy conscription, it was John Newton Sr. Everyone was a little afraid of his

father—a pompous and severe man with all the right connections and a distaste for injustice. The man always managed to get
his way . . . the son had been counting on that.

"Strip!" the captain commanded, and Newton never felt the
quartermaster's hands on his back, never heard the fabric rip, so
black was his rage and bitter his despair. Then all was suddenly,
eerily silent, and he heard the unmistakable *whisk* of the cat slip-
ping out of its red baize bag.

How many times had he stood with the other midshipmen
at forenoon, watching the cat o' nine unfurl onto the deck, horrified and fascinated at once? How many times had he winced
as the iron-studded tails flew through the air, connected with
skin, and raked down a sailor's back? And how many times had
he convinced himself that he could always talk his way out of
this kind of punishment?

Too, too many times.

But this time he'd realized much too late that no amount of
persuasion would stay the captain's hand. A war was on. Newton
had taken his leave without permission and been caught on the
road to Dartmouth. Now the captain was determined to make
an example of him.

"Do your duty," the captain told the boatswain's mate. And
Newton determined right then he would throw himself into the
sea. He would suffer this final humiliation, but when they
unbound him, he would put an end to his sorry life. And he
would take one or two of these meddlesome sailors with him.

He looked up, defiant and eager to choose his victim, but
found nothing there in the twilight—no sailors, no Marines, no
ship. He lay on the sand, his hot face pressed against the cool

planks of a small overturned boat, gripping the mooring rope, shaking from the fever. The scene that played over and over in his delirium was real. Close to a year had passed, but he *had* been flogged on board a man-of-war—he bore twelve cat's marks to prove it. He *had* stood and lurched toward the rail, but a bucket of salt water thrown across his lacerated back had sent him to his knees.

It was a memory too awful in its actuality to be a dream.

"Mr. Newton?" The slave they called Tome stepped into view and squatted beside him in the sand. "The princess say you are to come to her."

Newton would have snorted at that—the title the master's mistress used and the idea that he could actually walk across the island—if he had been capable of making any sound at all. As it was, he simply shook his head no.

"But you must come." Tome pried Newton's hand from the rope and slung it over his far shoulder. "She say she will have me whipped if I am back without you."

Newton felt himself hauled to his feet, the sudden change in position reinvigorating the blinding headache and muscle spasms he could manage only by lying perfectly still. Tome stood with him as his head lolled forward and he groaned in agony. Then a cup was pressed to his lips, and he smelled the wonderful fragrance of fresh water. He opened his mouth and savored the mouthful as he would the first glass of Christmas punch. He swallowed and took another mouthful, then another, and another. Then he opened his eyes and looked into the gentle face of Tome's island "wife"—a young, sturdy woman and holder of the cup. He opened his mouth for more, but she shook her head, tied the empty cup at her waist, and threw his other arm across her shoulders.

So this was how it would be. They would help or drag or carry him to their mistress. But he would go.

They started up the sloping beach, Newton trying to move his aching legs as they pulled him inland, around the dense coconut palms, and over the marshy ground. They did not rush, but neither did they tarry as they ushered him along, occasionally speaking to each other in their strange Krio language—a language Newton had just begun to learn when the fever had struck. They stopped for a moment, and the cup was again pressed to his lips. He drank and whispered, "Tenki ya." *Thank you*. He waited, hoping they would see he was just one of them—a slave to a cruel mistress on this miserable island . . . a supplicant for a drink of water. The cup touched his lips again.

Then on they trudged, each step familiar to him from his earliest days here after he'd been discharged to the merchant ship *Levant*—days when he'd worked as a free man alongside a powerful English trader . . . days, then months, filled with home building and rice planting, goods trading and slave selling. It was the Englishman's African mistress—the self-proclaimed "princess"—who'd eventually spoiled everything. Because Newton did not honor her status, he surmised, because he was a white man and confidant of her "husband," she'd developed a prejudice against him. She'd soon found her opportunity to exert her power when he'd become sick and missed the trader's trip up the Rio Nuñez. She'd made him a slave.

And now the tyrant commanded him to her side.

Soon they were in sight of the village guards, the little bit of water and exercise doing much for Newton's condition so that when they gained admittance and crossed the threshold of the "princess'" mud house, he was able to stand without assistance.

There she sat—the great Pey Ey—trying to look imperious in near-royal dining splendor. Her dark fleshy skin gleamed under the candlelight as she lorded over the lavish table, shoveling large spoonfuls of rich food into her painted mouth, barely chewing before washing it all down with a deep red wine.

He hated rich food—hated the way fresh vegetables slumped in heavy cream sauces and joints of beef sat smothered in fatty stock. That kind of fare simply encouraged greed. Give him a slice of buttered toast dotted with oysters wrapped in a rasher of bacon and grilled to crisp perfection. Give him the skewer, and he would pierce her gluttonous heart.

A servant leaned close to the "princess," refilling her crystal wineglass, whispering in her ear. She squinted over at her intruder, perching delicate gold spectacles on her wide nose— spectacles everyone knew she did not need but considered essential to appearing "learned."

"Meester Newton," she said in her haughty island accent. "Why do you inseest on playing the poor, seeckly beggar, hmm?"

He knew from past experience that he was not expected— indeed, should make no attempt—to answer, that it gave her great pleasure to mock him in the presence of her servants . . . that any rebuttal on his part would only earn him ill treatment. She sighed dramatically and beckoned to him, the fat of her upper arms wobbling and straining against the rows of shiny armlets that only enhanced her girth.

He did not think he had the strength to cross the room unaided, but he put one foot in front of the other, covering the short distance in a shuffle step, breathing heavily from the effort. When one of the many empty chairs was within reach, he made a grab for the high back, focusing on a strange spot on his tormentor's costume—an odd-shaped circle of gray out of sync with the intricate pattern of yellows and reds on her sari. He frowned.

She pounced on his expression. "You are very deesappointed you no longer share my table, Meester Newton?"

*She is stupid, as well as fat,* he thought. He missed sharing nothing with this bully.

She flicked her wrist over the exquisite silver and china. He followed the motion, taking in the enormous spread of food laid out in true European fashion, nearly swooning from the aromas that triggered his empty stomach to contract in sudden desperate need.

"You mees the lavish meals and conversation weeth my brother, no? You mees sparring weeth the Bombo keeng, yes?" She gestured to the chair he gripped. "Come. Seet. Speak to *me.*" He did not move, so she picked up her half-empty plate and offered it to him. "I am feenished, so you may have eet."

The fever may have muddled his mind, but it did not escape him that she was offering him her scraps, as she would offer them to a dog. Part of him was outraged—he was no dog. Part of him was humbled, as a beggar wanting alms. And he watched as, astonishingly, his eager hand reached out of its own volition, it seemed, and grasped the china plate. But no sooner did she release it than the weight of the platter proved too much. He watched in detached dismay as it slipped from his hand, flipped, and bounced on the floor, sending every morsel of food into the rushes covering the packed dirt.

He dropped to his knees as Pey Ey cackled with glee. Tears sprang to his eyes as he tried to gather up the soggy mess. But it was in vain. Gone. The first meal offered him in days was gone.

He looked up, blinking back the tears, and caught a distorted glimpse of himself in an ornate mirror leaning against the far wall. He stared back in horror. Who was this emaciated, filthy man with the ragged hair and blistered skin? In the candlelight he scarcely recognized his face—weirdly pinched and sickly yellow under a rat's nest of beard. His cheekbones strained against his skin, and each dull eye was circled with a bluish tinge. Where was the hearty Englishman of twenty who walked with a sailor's swagger and ridiculed without remorse? What had this mad, mad career done to him? He wagged his head side to side. And why was the son of a wealthy shipowner kneeling at the feet of a cruel and contemptuous African whore?

*Get up!* What remained of his ego screamed at him. *Get up!*

"Get up." Her foot came from under the table and caught him in the ribs. He gasped with the effort it took to resist the blow and remain on his hands and knees. When he did not comply with her command, strong hands grasped his upper arms and hauled him to his feet.

Pey Ey shouted something in Krio, and he was dragged out of the house and back through the trees to the slave quarters. Once through the cabin door, his captors became more gentle. They carefully lowered him onto his mat, and a kind hand placed his head on the log that now served as his pillow.

He closed his eyes. At least she had not ordered her servants to mimic him this time. At least they had not pelted him with limes as he'd staggered away. After the flogging on the *Harwich*, he thought he'd suffered cruelly at the hands of his shipmates—demoted, shunned, miserable in both flesh and spirit. But he had not been tormented. He had not been denied basic physical survival.

He closed his eyes, hoping to sleep but not dream, and saw Plymouth as he'd left it—the trees in spring leaf, the dockyard bustling with trade and shipbuilding, Mount Edgcumbe rising behind the city like a sentry. He'd stood on the deck of the *Harwich* that day and kept his eyes on the shoreline as they'd passed out of the sound and into the bay, then the Channel.

And before the shore had even faded from view, he'd been gripped with such a longing that he'd felt he would never breathe deeply again. For whilst his heart had certainly ached for the loss of hearth and home, it had been a sharper, more profound thing that had unexpectedly seized him. There was a time, long, long ago—before they'd taken his diseased mother out of the city, before she'd died that horrible death . . . a time when the days were filled with love and poetry and contemplation. The last time he had . . . *belonged* somewhere, to someone.

He thought he'd happened upon it again in a moment both fleeting and full of promise, in the home of his mother's last season . . . in the home of Mary Catlett. Mary . . . dear, sweet Mary of the ginger hair and blue, blue eyes, first a playful freckled girl, now a sparkling young woman. She'd made him think of a line from Virgil: "When I saw her, I was undone." She was the only element of innocence left in his depraved life, and he clung to the spirit of her memory, as he'd clung to his mother's skirt when she'd left him so many years ago.

Chatham . . . Wapping . . . Plymouth—all distant points of distant memories.

And here he now sprawled, neither sailor nor scholar, neither lover nor beloved, neither departing nor returning . . . just a slave on an African island, burning with fever, desperate for a cup of water.

He *would* recover, he promised himself. He would steal food, if he must, and regain muscle, and then he would invoke *lex talionis*—retaliation. And when he escaped, he would make certain that no one on this godforsaken island would ever forget the name *John Newton.*

# CHAPTER

## 2

*Chatham, Kent*
*January 1746*

S he hated good-byes.

They were rarely done well—the bidder proffering formal words of safety and good health and repressing emotions of either relief or sorrow at the parting; the leave-taker, his foot already in the stirrup, thinking less of what he was leaving and more of whence he came. Even with the best-laid plans, the parting seemed so abrupt and hurried, and within moments of the final wave and settling dust the regrets settled in.

Mary was listing her regrets as she watched the morning London-bound stage pull up to the coach office on High Street. Any moment now her brother would get on that stage. And she had not broached the topic with him—the topic only he knew still lay so heavily on her heart.

Last night, whilst Jack had regaled his friends with yet another tawdry tale of life as a junior monitor at boarding school, she had slipped out, unnoticed, searing into memory the sight and sound of her brother laughing with the Best boys. Almost the entire Christmas holiday had been filled with laughing—squeals from young George as Jack had carried him under his arm, room to room, as if George were a riding crop and not a wriggling three-year-old. She'd heard snickers from her father's den and chortles from her mother's kitchen. Only Elizabeth, feeling superior in her fifteen years to Jack's paltry fourteen, resisted the merriment.

Regret seemed misplaced in such a memory.

But here Mary sat, curled up in a heavy quilt on the window seat of her third-floor bedroom shortly before dawn, regretting. She gazed out at the dark winter sky, the oil lamps dotting the snow-covered street with pools of yellow light, illuminating the figures of night watchmen on patrol and travelers rushing toward the six-o'clock stage. From here, she would wordlessly ache and wish her brother a silent *adieu*.

She'd made a lot of wishes from this perch. The conversion of attic to living space had caused no amount of astonishment when she'd suggested it to her parents two years ago. Yes, she'd agreed, it was stuffy in the summer and frigid in the winter. But she simply loved the views from the dormer window. In the spring she pushed it open to let in the tangy ocean breezes. She could watch the far-off ships make their way into the harbor, the sails and flags flapping, the men gesturing and shouting to each other on the decks. In late fall she often watched the first snowflakes drift lazily by, saw the passersby glance up at the sky, heard them exclaim to each other, then hurry on. So much of life, so many smells and sounds, rode the wind to her little space.

Through this window she often imagined herself out on that sidewalk with her luggage, about to board the London stage . . . or on the arm of a certain naval officer, en route to a nearby party. In the world beyond the window she was more than the eldest daughter of a customs officer—she was a boy with worldly options in profession and adventure, she was the lady of the house, she belonged to someone. Outside the window she was not a lonely young woman of seventeen.

The town clock struck quarter of six, interrupting her reverie. Jack had not appeared in front of the coach office. What was her brother up to?

"I miss you every day."

Mary looked over her shoulder at Jack, leaning against the doorframe as if he had all the time in the world, smiling and so handsome in his dark traveling boots and cloak. She smirked back at him.

"You do not."

"But I do!" And his eyes twinkled with mischief. "I miss besting you at cards, and besting you at whistling, and besting you on that lame mare you spoil. The Bedford boys are much, much more of a challenge."

She tossed him what she hoped was a truly priggish look.

He smiled all the way to his eyes, then his mouth softened, and he cocked his head slightly. "Why will you not say goodbye to me, Mary?"

She turned back to the window. "'Parting is such sweet sorrow . . .'"

She heard the grimace in his voice. "Oh dear. You'll not be quoting Shakespeare to me on such a dreary morning. I shall go mad as Hamlet trying to place it in the right play, then the right act, then in the right character's mouth all the way past London."

She closed her eyes in exasperation. *"Hamlet?"*

"I shall go mad as . . . Macbeth?"

"No."

"Desdemona?"

She swung completely around until her feet hit the cold floor with a *thunk*. "Honestly, Jack. For twenty pounds a year one might think the professors of the great Bedford School would teach you *something* of the classics."

He stared at her silently until she sighed. "It is quite possibly one of the most famous refrains in all of literature."

He shook his head.

"It is from Act II, scene ii of the greatest of romantic trage-dies."

He shrugged his shoulders, and she stared hard at him. *"Juliet"*—she paused for the moment of recognition to dawn—"bids *Romeo* farewell until they meet again on the morrow. But they do not . . . meet again." And she frowned.

Jack slowly nodded his head, left the doorway, and sat next to her on the window seat. When he spoke, all the brotherly teasing had left his voice. When he spoke, he talked quietly, as a friend.

"So you've not heard from him again."

She shook her head.

*Him.* They no longer spoke his name, as Mum had forbidden the relationship and any further contact in person or by post.

But *he* had found a way to circumvent the order. Over the past year several envelopes addressed to "Mrs. Susannah Eversfield," her mother's sister, had mysteriously appeared in her saddlebags or reticule or volume of prose. Inside were clandestine letters written to "My Dear Mary" in a fluid hand. Letters signed by *him*—John Newton.

And then, just as suddenly and without explanation, the letters had stopped appearing.

She dared not question her aunt, for her complicity went unspoken between them. She scoured the papers in vain for mention of the HMS *Harwich* in either war with Spain or France. In desperation Mary had confided her worries in a letter to Jack. Her brother had powerful connections at Bedford School and considered John a friend.

Jack took her hand and spoke in a low voice. "You know that had I come with any information on the *Harwich* or John, I would have told you immediately."

She nodded, her head down, a lump in her throat.

Jack sighed. "War is a good and a terrible thing—and the Navy may be just the sort of employment to make him, well, *worthy* . . . at least in Mum's mind."

Mary sat there with her brother and dearest friend, fighting back the urge to tell him everything racing through her mind: Where was the *Harwich*—that massive, heavily armed warship? Was the Navy a good fit for someone of John's bookish disposition? Would the wars never end? Conflict was good for a royal dockyard such as Chatham . . . "Excellent for business," her father liked to remind them. When John returned, would he return to her? He traveled to exotic lands, full of intriguing women. Moreover, she was a young woman of marriageable age in a naval port bursting with eligible men . . . would she be free to receive him?

She turned toward Jack and drew a breath, ready to reveal her thoughts, when the watchman's stick thumped on the front door, his cry of "Good morrow, good morrow, my masters all!" interrupting them. Immediately afterward the coachman's whistle cut through the air, Mum called out, and Jack leapt to his feet.

"I must make haste." He kissed her quickly and dashed for the stairs. He turned at her door. "Do not lose hope." And then he was gone.

Hope.

She opened a door beneath the window seat and pulled out a volume of Shakespeare's sonnets. Pressed between numbers LXIV and LXV was a letter sent nearly a year ago from the town of Deal. There were other letters hidden within the pages of other books. But this was the letter that sustained her when worry overpowered faith.

She unfolded it, her eyes traveling a familiar path to the middle of the page.

*The first day I saw you I began to love you.*

Bold, heart-stopping words written in a careful hand on a sheet of plain white paper. Affectionate words—whole sentences—preceded and followed that statement. Indeed, the letter was an entire page of genuine regard. But this was the sentence Mary read again and again . . . the sentence that made her heart beat more steadily, the declaration that kept real fear at bay.

She tried to imagine John as he'd written those words aboard the *Harwich*. She pictured him in his nankin breeches and blue jacket, surprisingly well-tailored for his tall frame. His tarpaulin hat would be cocked just so as he worked the middle watch, putting pen to paper in the relative quiet of night. Even in the dead of winter, his face would have the sailor's color of life amidst the elements.

His was not a handsome face, Mary reflected. It was long and had too many sharp angles—very Romanesque. But she found his countenance quite pleasing, and the shock of his blue eyes against deeply tanned skin was captivating. He'd eschewed the powdered wig, thankfully, and kept his auburn hair clipped short.

When she'd last seen him, a year ago Christmas—when she'd had an inkling of his growing affection, when she'd learned of their mothers' matchmaking—she'd been uncharacteristically girlish, combining their adult features into sons and daughters, painting imaginary portraits, daring to think of herself as part of a striking pair. Those images, combined with the letters, had created an expectation she found difficult to surrender—even in the harsh reality of daylight.

Reality reared its head as the watchman's fading knock and cry drifted into her fantasy, the smell of toasting bread wafted up the stairs, and the coachman whistled again, cracking the whip over the horses' backs.

Mary stood, threw off the quilt, and marched to her wardrobe. She donned a robe of worsted wool dyed red—the color of courage, she resolved. A life with John Newton was possible. She believed it. Jack believed it. That was enough assurance for now.

She stepped into her slippers and descended into the rooms of their first acquaintance, remembering the past, anticipating the future. *Aristotle was right,* she thought. *Hope is a waking dream.*

# CHAPTER

## 3

*Plantain Islands*
*April 1746*

N ewton watched from his hidden vantage point as Tome set out for the English ship anchored a quarter mile off-shore, the first to arrive in three months. In the slave's satchel was a bundle of correspondence. And in that bundle were two clandestine letters—one addressed to John Newton Sr. of the Royal Africa Company and, within its folds, one to Mary Catlett of Chatham, Kent.

He didn't care if his father read his passionate words to Mary and shook his head in displeasure. He didn't care about anything anymore but getting off this island. And only the letter in the satchel could achieve that.

Newton cursed the European traders who stayed on board their ship, inaccessible to him, fearing the tsetse fly, the river blindness, the Guinea worm, or any one of the deadly diseases that claimed half of the men sent to "the white man's grave" on the African shore. He cursed them but understood their fear, for hadn't *he* just managed to survive the fever? If anyone called his present state surviving . . .

He watched as Tome steadily rowed the canoe out to the massive ship, his rhythmic paddling setting a line of verse through Newton's head.

*Beware and take care of the gulf of Benin,*
*For the one that comes out there are forty goes in.*

Round and round the sea shanty traipsed in his mind as little by little the boat grew smaller. He closed his eyes and tried to shake the verse. But it just grew louder in protest.

He was going mad. Hunger—relentless, gnawing hunger—was slowly driving him mad.

He lurched to his feet and made his way, tree by tree, to a remote corner of the island. Euclid was there. Euclid would help him.

He passed the lime grove he'd worked so hard to improve these months, barely glancing at the young trees he'd planted exactly twelve feet apart. He would never live long enough to taste their fruit or feel them pound against his ribs, thrown from tormenting hands. That knowledge left him indifferent.

He stumbled around the bamboo-like stems of the cassava, envisioning their roots and remembering what that fleshy sub-stance had done to him last night. His bile rose in painful recol-lection. He might as well have taken tartar emetic, so completely had his stomach emptied. But he would dig up the root and eat it again if need be. He could not know when a stranger or a slave in chains might again take pity and pass a bit of food to him.

Then, just ahead, he heard the unmistakable sound of a coconut falling. He hurried as fast as his emaciated frame could take him toward the noise, visually cracking the nut open, drinking the watery milk, tasting the white pulpy meat, rationing himself if he could, feasting on it for days. The tearing hunger would subside enough to let him sleep through the night. He could gain a little strength and be useful again. He could earn a real meal.

He arrived at the tree just in time to see a slave boy snatch the coconut from the ground. They locked eyes—the boy frowning, seeming to mull over the consequences of relinquishing his find, Newton trying to convey his need. Slowly Newton held out his hand. *Give it to me,* he silently pled. *Let me eat.* The boy hesitated, then turned with his coconut and ran.

Newton's hand dropped to his side. In just moments the island returned to its regular cruel rhythm. The relentless wind whistled through the trees, rustling the fronds, the sea rolled onto the sand, the birds chattered. He stood at the site of his lost meal and felt nothing—not disappointment, not anger. He felt . . . dead.

Oh, that it were true.

He mustered a little strength and trod on to the shore, around the place where he washed his shirt—his only shirt—in darkness, past the stone where he laid out his handkerchief and length of cloth in the pounding rain. He came upon the familiar outcropping of rock, reached into a slit, withdrew a packet, and collapsed with it onto the sand. The journey to this point had exhausted him.

He leaned his head back against the rock and closed his eyes. He was so weary. Ever so softly his mother's voice came to him, as if on the sea breeze . . . *"Come unto me, all ye that labour and are heavy laden—"*

*No!* He surged to his feet, dizzy with the effort. He shook his head—shook away the voice, shook away the Scripture. That was a promise of his mother's God, not his father's . . . not his. There was no rest, not for the wicked, not for the bondsman. And there was no God.

He focused on the packet in his hand and pulled the string that held the palm leaves closed. Inside was his last purchase in Plymouth—Euclid's *Elements*. He ran his fingers across the book's cover.

Geometry. There was a harmony to the discipline of mathematics. Everything existing in life—every tangible thing with a surface—could be defined by curves and angles and worked into the absolutes of parts and wholes and proportions. One did not have to rely upon an elusive and indefinable divinity for peace. One simply calculated.

Newton pulled a long stick from the rocks and began to outline ratios and proportions from Book V. He dragged his stick through the sand, measuring out triangles and squares, proving complicated propositions and chains of deductions, drawing and whispering all the while, "... $m(x_1 + x_2 + ... + x_n) = m\,x_1 + m\,x_2 + ... + m\,x_n\,...$"

He worked his proofs until the sun began to set and the familiar cramping bent him over with pain. He leaned heavily on his stick. Perhaps Euclid would speak to him from the grave and give him the formula to determine longitude. Then he'd just approach Parliament, render John Harrison's sea clock obsolete, collect his prize money, and propose to Mary. Simple. He wanted to laugh at his own desperate wit but couldn't.

Instead, he looked across the shoreline and saw his renderings for what they were—geometric scribbles by an outcast, a beggar, a servant of slaves on an African island.

And this time when his mother's voice gently pushed against the door of his closed mind, he let it in . . . for on this occasion, her Scriptures spoke the truth.

*"O wretched man that I am."*

# CHAPTER

## 4

*Chatham, Kent*
*April 1746*

T he hand pressed over her mouth was so tight, Mary could
taste blood. Her own hand flew up, trying to pry the
other away, when her mother spoke ever so softly.

"Mary. Calm yourself."

The attic room was inky black in the foggy, moonless night,
but the voice was unmistakably her mother's. Mary slowed her
breathing, and the hand moved away. She sat up.

"Mum?"

A finger came back to her lips, signaling silence. Her mother
leaned close.

"Put on these breeches and shirt—they belong to Jack."

Mary felt the worn fabric pressed into her hands.

"Hurry. Light no candles—button them from memory. Find me in the kitchen."

Her mother left as silently as she'd come, and Mary sprang into action, throwing off her linen shift and pulling on the soft breeches, attaching the front "fall," fumbling with the buckle just below the knee. As she transformed from girl into boy, it dawned on her that her mother's comment of "button them from memory" could only mean that the years of secret exploits with Jack and the Best boys had not been so secret after all. Hmm. She would think on this later.

She felt her way down the steep attic steps, then crept down the back stairs in her stockings, careful to avoid the steps that creaked. She emerged into the kitchen, and in a thrice her hand was at her throat where a gasp lodged.

Before the cooking fire, sprawled in a chair, was her father . . . his shirt covered in blood. Her mother stood over him, trickling spoonfuls of rum into his mouth, murmuring to him as his hands alternately shook and gripped the chair arms.

"Mum?" The word came out on a panicked breath, and her mother turned her head sharply, frowning.

"Stay where you are, Mary." She moved to block her daughter's view, her dressing gown billowing out and around her. "Look behind you, on the hook there."

Mary turned and found one of Jack's old waistcoats. She drew it on over the ruffled shirt, expertly pulling the tight sleeves into position and buttoning the front only at the waist. On another hook was an old-fashioned Monmouth, somewhat battered but still an acceptable hat. She put it on over her braided hair, pulling it low. The greatcoat came last, the expanse of it hiding her feminine frame and the collar covering her braid. She turned back toward the fire.

Her mother eyed her critically, then spoke in hushed and measured tones. "Your father has been injured in a smuggling raid. You need to make your way, as quickly and quietly as possible, to the number three house at The Terrace. Do you know it?"

Mary nodded her head.

"Speak only to the Marine officer who lives there—not the servant at the door, not the housekeeper. When he comes to you, speak one word: Blake. He should follow you without question."

*Blake . . . the great admiral, Robert Blake,* Mary presumed. She nodded again.

"Pistols . . ." The pain-filled word floated up from the chair, and her mother hesitated a moment, then retrieved a brace of flintlock pistols from the greatcoat on the floor. She handled each one with precision—plunging the ramrod into the barrel to assure the roundball was still packed in tightly, pulling back on the pommel to check the gunpowder in the priming pan. Satisfied, she stepped a little forward and held them out.

Mary crossed the short distance and took them, noting her mother's pale hands streaked with blood—the blood she'd tasted on waking . . . her father's blood. She looked up into her mother's questioning gaze.

"You know how to use these?"

Mary nodded.

"Jack?"

Mary withheld the answer to that query, reluctant to implicate her brother and coconspirator.

Her mother sighed and waved a hand. "Never mind. We shall speak of all this"—she flicked her fingers up and down Mary's boy-dressed form—"another time."

Mary stowed the pistols inside her coat and waited for any last instructions.

Her mother spoke low. "I cannot stress how important it is that you not be caught and questioned on this mission. It is why I have given you so little information. Stay to the back streets. Speak to no one . . . but hurry."

A cough and then the word, "Hawthorn . . ." came from the chair.

Her mother shook her head. "Of course. The watchword tonight is 'hawthorn.'" She stared hard at her daughter. "But you will not need it, Mary. The watchmen will not see you."

Mary nodded her understanding and hastened to the heavy and windowless back door, bending to pull on her black riding boots. As she crossed the threshold, she looked over her shoulder at her mother—back at her task, trickling rum between her husband's chattering teeth. Mary closed the door with a gentle *click*.

The sky was dark and thick with fog. She walked by instinct through the walled garden, over the smooth stones, past the poppies and foxgloves she could not see, until she reached the gate. This was the tricky part. The gate creaked with annoying consistency unless one pulled and lifted it up . . . just . . . so . . . And she was onto the side street without a sound.

She kept to the alleyways as she calculated her route. The Terrace was less than two miles due north of High Street. As she and the boys had taken a similar path more times than her mother wanted to know, she figured she could make her way there in less than thirty minutes at a good trot. The fog would make it interesting.

She worked her way toward Brook Street, letting her mind wander over tonight's events. The sight of her father, shaking and bloodied, had been unnerving—the cat-and-mouse games between customs officers and smugglers had clearly turned deadly. But she was more surprised at her mother's conduct. Was this the lady of tea-table gossip and embroidery, the very model of femininity and grace? The sight of Elizabeth Catlett "née Churchill," as she liked to remind people, handling a pistol with ease had rendered the daughter speechless. And this vocal opponent of female higher education and worldly advancement had a startling familiarity with passwords and military personnel. Either tonight's situation was extraordinary, or Mary did not really know her mother. She suspected it was the latter.

An expanse of muddy road loomed before her, and she guessed she had arrived at Brook Street. She listened for a moment, then dashed across it, thankful for the fog cover, and made for the Military Burial Ground—the favored destination of the boys' late-night jaunts. She trotted toward it with confidence, noting the eerie outlines, smiling in spite of her sober mission.

Turning northeast, she skidded to a halt and drew a pistol. The unmistakable sound of human voices drifted toward her from the burial ground's edge. She crouched low and waited, turning right and left on the balls of her feet. Silence. She crept forward, listening, and caught the unmistakable sound of . . . giggling—girls giggling. She pocketed the gun and shook her head. What were a band of girls doing out so late at night?

And then she remembered the date: April 30, the eve of May Day. That was the reason for the password "hawthorn"—the flowering branch was fondly called "may." And that was what drew impressionable girls outside tonight. She hung her head in disgust of silly girls everywhere . . . girls impressed by folklore claiming that if you sat beneath a tree on this night, you might see the Queen of the Fairies ride by on her snow-white horse or hear the sound of her horse's bells. Then she might lure you away to Fairyland for seven years. Jack would have loved this opportunity. Mary could only think that the girls' presence would cost her valuable time.

The voices sounded close—too close—so she abandoned her eastern route and cut west through the grounds, then northeast again past the Sailors' Home. She became disoriented in the expanse of land beyond the Home and was turning about, trying to get her bearings, when the bells of St. Mary's Church began to chime. *Dong . . . dong . . . dong . . .* rang the bells. Three o'clock. She had not checked the time at her departure, but she knew instinctively that she had used up her thirty minutes.

She moved toward the fading sound, skirted St. Mary's, and arrived at one end of The Terrace, a long row of three-story town homes surrounded by cast-iron fencing. She slunk around to the back alley and approached from the rear. Once there, she chided herself for her error—no house numbers adorned the garden gates, and she could not see the back stoops for the fog. She could be at number three or third from the last.

She crept around again to the front, scurrying along the side-walk, squinting through the haze at the houses. *Where* were the numbers? A horse whinnied not twenty yards up the street, and Mary tore back the way she'd come, spying an ornate $\mathcal{N\!o}\ 1$ on the corner fence just as she disappeared into the fog.

*Stay calm . . . almost there,* she told herself as she returned to the alley. She counted off the gates, lifted the handle to number three, and stepped into a moist and fragrant patch of spring growth. She made her way along a shrouded brick path, inhaling the unmistakable essence of jasmine and chamomile, wondering at the sort of Marine officer who would design such an oasis.

Her boot slammed into the stoop, and she went down hard on the heels of her hands, skimming the top step with her chin. She pushed herself up fast, examining her skinned and, doubtless, bleeding palms, irritated that she had not worn gloves. She was turning her stinging hands side to side, squinting in the foggy darkness, when the door banged open.

In the doorway, wigless and partially dressed, a heavy tumbler of a dark liquid in one hand, a cocked pistol in another, stood the biggest Marine Mary had ever seen. In silhouette from the soft light behind him, he looked positively menacing. She gaped, openmouthed.

The Marine raised the glass to his lips. "This cannot be good tidings."

Mary stared at the man, her mother's instructions ringing in her ears. *"Speak one word . . ."*

"Blake," Mary finally said, clear and low.

The glass stopped midair, and the Marine spewed a string of curse words that would have made every Tory in Parliament blush. He lowered the pistol and shook his head. "Wait there," he ordered and marched back through the house.

Mary stood stock-still at the back stoop, her skinned hands forgotten, her frantic mind in a whirl. It occurred to her, for the first time since she'd crept through her garden, that this was no mere adventure. Something dangerous and terrible had happened tonight—something that required the utmost secrecy and involved a high-ranking Marine.

*You are Jack,* she told herself. *You are a fearless, daring boy.* She jumped when a leather pouch landed at her feet.

"Belt it over your shoulder," the Marine ordered, ramming a Brown Bess into his musket sling.

Mary complied, slightly less terrified to see the Marine in the familiar red jacket over his linen breeches and now-buttoned shirt. She watched as he threw a haversack over his shoulder, then snatched a cropped cap off the inside wall and settled it over his queued wig.

He turned to her and yanked on the pouch belted over her waistcoat. "You will not lose this. Do you understand?"

He was inches from her face, and she nodded, wide-eyed.

"Excellent. Now, where do you take me?"

"H-High Street, sir."

The Marine shook his head and cursed again. "He is badly wounded?"

"Y-Yes . . . I believe so."

"Musket or sword?"

"I do not know, sir."

"Then we must hurry." And he started down the garden path, never looking to see that she followed.

He was through the gate and down the alley in full stride, and Mary knew she'd have to trot to keep him in sight in this fog. She followed him to St. Mary's, where he turned onto Church Hill, then Military Road, taking the most direct and visible route at a grueling pace.

She was three yards behind him, panting for breath, when a voice called out.

"Who goes there?"

The Marine halted and Mary crashed into him. He reached back, grabbed the front of her waistcoat, and threw her into the ditch beside the road.

"Captain Mathias Ward of the Royal Marines," he replied.

Mary watched him ease the Brown Bess from the sling and brace the butt against his shoulder. She'd landed on her stomach, grabbing at the tall grass to hold her position, the scrapes on her hands smarting at the contact.

A watchman stepped into view. "Yer pardon, sir. Rumor is the Hawkhurst gang is about. We're advising folk ta lob low 'til arter the fog lifts."

The Marine lowered the musket and shifted his stance to block his companion from view.

"The smugglers took to city streets? Whatever for?"

"Well, sir . . ." The watchman spat on the road. "Rumor is they was ambushed and shot a man—prob'ly milit'ry. They'll be tryin' ta run 'im ta ground, finish 'im off 'n 'ang 'im fer 'is trouble."

"Well, then," the Marine said cheerfully, returning the musket to its sling and throwing his arm across the watchman's shoulder, "I'll walk with you along your route 'til we reach High Street. What do you say to that?"

Mary lay in the ditch, listening to their voices fade into the fog. The gang had shot her father and pursued him into town. They might be outside her house now—and she had the pistols.

When two minutes had passed and she heard nothing but night sounds, she climbed out of the ditch, found the pouch still firmly in place, and followed the road to Medway, cutting through alleyways until she reached High Street. She listened for the Marine and the watchman, heard nothing, and dashed across, suddenly exhausted and ready for the adventure to end.

In a thrice she was at her garden gate, closing it soundlessly. She dashed down the path and burst through the kitchen door just as the Marine drew a knife and advanced on her father.

In one swift movement Mary was between the men, one pistol drawn and cocked. As if from a distance, she heard her mother shout, "No!" But she could not remember a time she'd been so ruthlessly determined.

The Marine stopped midstride, holding up the knife and his free hand, one eyebrow raised in question.

"Let him come, child," her father panted from his chair. "He is . . . a physician."

Mary's eyes widened, but she held her position. The situation grew more incredible by the minute. She considered the evidence—the urgency . . . the precious pouch . . . the questions about her father's wounds. As the moment stretched, she reluctantly acknowledged that no matter her own apprehension, her father trusted this man, so she must trust him. For now. She uncocked the pistol but kept it at her side.

The Marine advanced to the fire and thrust the knife over the flames, turning it back and forth, his back not quite to the room.

Her father coughed and drew a noisy breath. "She is just . . . like her brother."

The Marine spun around and stared at Mary in astonishment. *"She?"*

Mary reached up and removed her hat, then pulled her long braid around to the front.

The Marine shook his head. "Well, I'll be—"

"Mama-a!" Young George's piercing cry gave them all a jolt, and her mother hurried to the back stairs, beckoning. "Mary—"

But the Marine cut her off. "Let the girl stay. I could use another pair of hands."

They faced off—Elizabeth Catlett née Churchill and the Marine captain, who saw by the narrowed eyes and set of the woman's chin that he had overstepped his authority in this house.

"I beg of you, madam," he hastily added and inclined his head.

At length her mother nodded and disappeared up the stairs as young George cried out again.

Mary turned to the Marine, who was wigless again and all business, pulling linen-wrapped bundles out of his haversack and placing them across a small table. Satisfied with their arrangement, he marched to the back door, pulling off his coat and hanging it on a hook.

"Off with your coats then, miss. And roll up your shirt sleeves. This is ghastly work."

She obeyed, hanging Jack's clothes on the hooks where she'd found them in what seemed like hours ago, folding her cuffs to above her elbows. Then she carried the pouch and pistol back over to her father's chair.

The Marine had pulled a worktable close to the fire and now bent over the injured man. "Here we go, Catlett," he said and, in an instant, lifted his patient out of the chair and had him on the table, as if he weighed no more than a child. George Catlett was not a tall man, but forty-five years of a hearty appetite had left its mark.

Mary watched in alarm as her father's eyes rolled back into his head. And then he passed out.

"Best to do painful work without warning," said the Marine and began to pull away the bloody fabric on the man's shoulder, cursing without restraint as he pulled and cut and probed until the entire section was exposed. He shook his head and looked over at his wary assistant.

"Are you strong?"

Mary nodded but moved no closer.

"The musket ball is next to the bone. I can get it with the forceps, but you'll have to hold him down."

Mary put down the pouch and pistol, walked to the table, and placed her hands on her father's chest.

The Marine grabbed her by the shoulders, forcing her down, talking all the while. "Put your forearm against his collarbone, and reach across him with your other arm. Grab the edge of the table and put all your weight into it. I'll be quick, but the pain is something terrible."

No sooner did Mary brace herself than her father's body jolted and he moaned in agony.

"Hold on," coaxed the Marine as Mary gripped the table,

her injured hand throbbing with the contact, her muscles straining. And then her father's body went limp. She stayed in position, waiting for the next order.

"Almost there."

And she heard the *clink* as the musket ball landed in a pewter
cup.

"Open the pouch," he ordered.

Mary dragged herself across her father and reached for the
leather bag. She opened it, surprised at the contents.

"Find the package labeled 'chamomile' and a small jar of
salve."

She sorted through the pouch, pushing aside rose oil and
spearmint, cumin and tobacco, until she located the items, then
turned to the Marine. She blanched as she watched him pull out
pieces of fabric and splinters of wood from her father's bleeding
shoulder.

He worked fast, probing and pulling, pushing against the
main artery, and coaching her along.

"Now I want you to mix a tablespoon of the chamomile and
a quarter cup of the salve into a nice paste." She didn't reply and
he glanced up at her, weaving on her feet, mouth slack from the
sight of the blood and open wound.

"Mary!"

She blinked and stared at the Marine, shocked at the sound
of her Christian name barked at her by a stranger in her own
kitchen.

"Make the ointment. Keep moving. I will call you over here
when I need you."

She moved to the counter and pulled a spoon from the

drawer, her hands shaking with the effort. She measured the chamomile and paste into a little bowl and stirred it with effort, her hands feeling hot and swollen.

The Marine continued to talk in a soothing, conversational manner.

"I'm tying off the arteries, then we'll apply the salve. The natives prefer slippery elm, but I think chamomile is a more elegant solution. Or maybe rose oil, also good for—"

"Headaches," Mary interjected, turning around.

The Marine nodded. "That it is." He glanced her way. "Find me a nice slice of bread, will you, Miss Catlett?"

She walked to the sideboard and found the bread.

"I want you to wet it down and spread the ointment over it, just like you would butter. Then I want you to warm it over the fire—not toast it, just get it nice and warm. Can you do that?"

She nodded and followed his instructions, feeling her head clear as she worked.

The Marine kept up the conversation. "If we were in the Americas, I'd have your father in a sweat bath tomorrow afternoon. Never seen anything like it to heal a man."

Mary slipped the bread into a long-handled pan and held it close to the fire. "You have lived with the natives in the Americas?"

"Oh yes. Quite an adventure, the Americas."

"And this is where you have learned so much about healing with herbs?"

"Yes."

"And you travel with the Navy on these voyages?"

"Yes."

"And you talk with the captains of these ships?"

The Marine was silent for so long that Mary turned to look at him, the smell of warm chamomile wafting over her. He was bent over the wound, pressing against the skin with both hands.

"Bring me the bread."

She brought the pan to the table and watched as he placed the entire slice, salve-side down, over the wound, tore away the crusts, then bound it with a long strip of cotton. He tied off the bandage, and she set down the pan, slowly flexing her fingers.

"Show me your hands."

Mary hesitated, then walked toward him, holding her hands out over her father's body.

The Marine looked at the scraped and swollen skin, sighed, and reached for the pouch.

"The ditch?"

"Your back stoop."

"Ah." He tore another strip of cotton and mixed a measure of rose oil and salve on the fabric. "What do you wish to know about the Navy, Miss Catlett?"

She watched him spread the salve back and forth along the cotton, the scent of the rose oil rising above the stench of blood-soaked clothing.

"Do you know of the HMS *Harwich*?"

He nodded. "The warship bound for the West Indies? Of course. Captain Carteret is a good friend."

"What . . . has become of it?"

"The captain completed his Africa mission and is now fulfilling his obligations in India."

"I see." She frowned. Then why had she not heard from John?

He applied the bandage to her left hand, the salve stinging and soothing at the same time. She watched him work on the second bandage.

"Do you . . . correspond with the captain of the *Harwich*?"

"Yes."

She hesitated. What she was about to ask was improper in the extreme. But propriety had fled the moment she'd donned her brother's clothes and gone unaccompanied to the Marine's house.

"I wonder if you would ask him about a particular sailor—a midshipman named Newton. John Newton."

The Marine applied the second bandage to her left hand, tying it off with a double knot. He met her eyes as her father stirred.

"You will come with your father to my garden every week and learn about the healing powers of herbs."

She blinked at him.

"In exchange I will write to the captain of the HMS *Harwich* and inquire about a sailor named John Newton."

She bit her lip and looked at her father.

"Do we have a deal, Miss Catlett?"

She dragged her gaze back to the Marine. He was still a terrifying man. But he might just be an answer to her most fervent prayers. She nodded.

"We have a deal."

# CHAPTER

## ⊰ 5 ⊱

*May Day*

I n the dream she was smiling, her mouth wide and almost aching with delight. In the dream she was a child again—still small enough to be carried in from the coach and placed, drowsy and contented, in her soft, soft bed. And men were not on warships . . . smuggling gangs were not terrorizing the coast . . .

Mary felt herself emerging from the dream and fought with every ounce of her subconscious to stay in that happy place. But the conscious won and her eyelids flickered open to half-light and reality.

She lay on the chaise lounge of the guest bedroom, wrapped in a coverlet and her dressing gown, her hands pressed together under her cheek. Her father lay in exactly the same position they'd placed him close to dawn—on his side, his injured shoulder propped up with a stack of heavy blankets. She watched his chest rise and fall as he breathed deeply in sleep, his face no longer contorted in pain or pale and slack in collapse. She was afraid last night that they—she, her mother, and the Marine— and not the bullet would finally kill him as they lugged him up the stairs and placed him, sweating and moaning, upon the unmade bed.

Her mother had sent her away to change out of Jack's clothes, and when she'd returned, minutes later, her father was undressed and tucked tightly into position, and the Marine was gone. They'd agreed that Mary would tend to her father— "taken ill in the night," they would say—whilst Elizabeth kept the children entertained with the goings-on of May Day.

When the door clicked shut behind her mother, Mary collapsed onto the chaise. Her head was spinning with the secrecy and drama of the night, and she thought she could not possibly rest. But she laid her head on the rose-patterned pillow and was asleep in moments.

Now the linen drapes let in just enough sunlight to make the yellow walls glow. She'd always loved this room. Sometimes a guest room, sometimes a back parlor, it felt . . . private, tucked away and looking out onto the garden. Many, many memories danced within the room—children's tea parties impersonating the adults' in the front parlor, afternoon naps with her visiting grandmother, and, of course, her first real conversation with John.

Mary turned onto her back. She had been curled up right here on this chaise lounge, midday, reading through a treasured copy of Handel's *Messiah*. So intent was she on the oratorio that she did not at first see him standing in the hall. Only when she heard the sharp intake of breath did she look up and into his stricken face.

Snow dusted the front and sleeves of his unfashionable brown frock coat. He was, undoubtedly, Jack's latest snowball victim, come to gain a reprieve by the fire.

"Do come in," she had said, imitating her mother's most generous tone.

But he had not moved from his spot. He'd simply said, "She died . . . here?"

She immediately understood he spoke of his mother's illness. She knew it seemed unimaginable to him—the room was dressed as a parlor . . . cozy, fragrant, and festooned with Christmas garlands. It was not the tightly sealed sickroom of a young woman wasting away from consumption.

"I was only four years old," she'd said, "but I remember her."

He looked right at her then.

"They were more than cousins, our mothers. They were like sisters. They had the same name, and I would try it out in secret." She smiled at him, but he did not return it.

"I liked to stand in the garden and look in on her. Her bed was here, by the windows."

His eyes cut to the heavy damask drapes thrown open to the winter sun. He opened his mouth several times to speak and finally uttered, "Was she . . . At the end, did she . . ."

Mary shook her head. "They did not speak of it—not to the children. But I remember Mum crying . . . and the wisteria in bloom."

He'd backed away then—away from the room, away from her.

Mary lay on the chaise, three years later, lingering with the memory. Ten words. That's all he'd uttered to her then and was the average length of any conversation directed toward her since. Theirs was a courtship without words—at least, without the spoken kind. If not for the letters, she would be completely unaware of his devotion.

"How long?"

The words croaked out of her father's throat, and she rushed to his side, a spoonful of water ready at his lips. He sipped several spoonfuls, then asked again.

"How long?"

She knew what he meant and looked toward the fireplace. The clock on the mantel had stopped and no one had bothered to wind it. She shook her head just as the town clock began to chime. They listened together.

"Eleven o'clock." She smiled, and he frowned.

"What . . . day?"

"'Tis May Day, Papa." She spooned more water into his mouth. *"Keep him hydrated,"* the Marine had told her. "And a good thing, too. Mum could take everyone away without a barrage of questions." She winked at him. "But you are left with me."

He smiled a little and spoke with difficulty. "Your mother . . . has a gift . . . for strategy."

*Among other things,* she thought, and put the backs of her fingers to his forehead. Warm . . . too warm. "You must rest. We will talk later." She turned away and was surprised at his grip on her hand.

"I want . . . to talk to you."

Mary knew this moment would come but had hoped for a small reprieve. The sigh escaped before she could stop it. "All right. But you must drink more water. Do we have a deal?"

The words were a harsh echo of last night's hasty agreement with the Marine. She tried to shake off her unease as she perched on the side of the bed and poured more water into a cup.

"Jack," her father began, "told me everything." Her surprise and dismay must have shown, for he patted her knee. " 'Tis good for a woman . . . to defend herself."

She considered that as she put the spoon to his lips. "As Mum can clearly do?"

He swallowed, then smiled and nodded. "Society is not yet ready . . . for Catlett women."

She noted the measure of pride that crept into his voice and relaxed a little.

"Last night . . ." He drew a deep breath. "The revenue cutters, the Navy dragoons, the Marines . . . all were involved in a plan to break the Hawkhurst gang." He licked his dry lips. "Once and for all."

She nodded and reached for the ointment on the bedside table. "Blake?" She patted the creamy mixture onto his mouth.

He rubbed his lips together. "A great strategist. Oh, that we had him this century."

She let him ponder that as she pressed more water onto him.

He swallowed. "Captain Ward"—he caught her eye—"the Marine you nearly shot, was against the plan from the start."

She frowned at the reminder and dropped her eyes.

"He did not trust our informant." Her father sighed. "He was right. We were outfoxed."

Mary felt this could be the right moment to approach her father about the deal she'd cut with the Marine—the deal that might locate John.

"Captain Ward is quite . . ." She searched for a word other than "terrifying."

"Scares the devil out of most men," her father supplied.

"Yes. Well, he has quite a knowledge of medicinal herbs—gained from the colonies, he says."

He nodded.

"I assisted him with your wound, and—"

He grabbed the hand holding the spoon, turning it over and revealing the bandage just under her sleeve. "I did this to you?" Such self-reproach in his tone.

She rushed to assure him. "No-no. Just a scrape, Papa."

"Show me."

He did not appear to believe her, so she pulled at the knot on her wrist and released the bandage. The scent of roses wafted up from her palm as he turned it side to side. The skin already looked improved, and the sting was long gone.

"No gloves," she admitted and shrugged. "I was in a bit of a hurry."

He grimaced.

She retied the bandage and returned to her topic. "With your permission, Captain Ward would like to instruct me in medicinal herbs."

"I know."

Mary was astonished at this and was at a loss on how to proceed. She sat in silence, waiting. Her father closed his eyes, clearly exhausted, his voice hoarse from this small exchange.

"He will honor his agreement . . . so you must honor yours."

She eased off the bed, ready to leave him in peace, but he opened his eyes and reached for her.

"Send a message. We shall come to him in two days' time."

"Papa . . . you are—"

He cut her off with a wave of his hand, then relaxed again. "I must be on my feet by the fifth of May."

She shook her head in confusion.

"The *Somerset* . . ." he whispered, fading. "They lay down the keel on Monday. I must . . . be there."

She watched him relax into sleep, then tiptoed out of the room. She would never understand men and their warships. But she understood duty. She stepped into her mother's private office, retrieving quill, ink, and paper from the desk, then made her way to the kitchen, composing the note to Captain Ward in her head.

Last night had been an adventure, she allowed. But she knew with almost certainty it would be the encounter two days hence that would change her life forever.

# CHAPTER

## 6

*The Financial District, London*
*Late June 1746*

The Master pounded on the pulpit to start the news' first
reading as the waiters they called "kidneys" dashed
through the smoky room in their navy blue livery, sliding cups
of tea and coffee across tables rubbed to a shine. The place was
packed, the din remarkable at eight o'clock on Friday morning.
And Joseph Manesty loved it.

There was nowhere in London quite like Lloyd's Coffee
House. Once a month he would leave his home and his lavender
bushes and make the two-day journey across the Irish Sea to the
English Channel to this bastion of maritime news and rumor. At
times he would linger in the captain's section—though he was
no longer a captain—or huddle in a corner, discussing figures
with other merchants. But as a rule he liked to sit in the center

of it all, perusing the *List* and *Gazette*, switching between coffee, tea, and sherbet, basking in the madness of marine commerce.

In his powdered wig and silk stockings, he looked every bit the successful shipowner he was. He managed a small fleet of vessels from his Liverpool headquarters, selecting officers and crew, equipping, stowing, and charting each craft. But in his heart of hearts, he was still the young and daring captain, commanding a company of men, rising swiftly and coolly to a myriad of seafaring crises. Some mornings of late he'd awoken, surprised to be on terra firma and—worse—in his midforties. His greatest dilemma at present involved avoiding the Spaniards in the ongoing War of Jenkins' Ear.

He sighed, but it was an expression of mostly peaceful sentiment. He was lounging in a coffeehouse on Lombard Street, surrounded by crises in the making. He did not need one of his own to be contented.

By ten o'clock Manesty had read his papers, made the rounds of booths to lay off his shipping risk, and entered a raffle for a horse. He caught a kidney as he raced by, ordering another coffee, and tried to relax in his chair, watching the door.

His real business at Lloyd's this day was an urgent meeting called by John Newton. He'd known the man for twenty-five years—stood by him when he'd captained for the East India Company, when he'd gained, lost, and gained again a wife, when he'd retired from the sea to agent for the Royal Africa Company.

He knew the man no one else knew.

Whilst others thought Newton a harsh and unfriendly sort, Manesty viewed his friend as firm and reserved. Newton was well-thought-of for his business sense—on that, everyone agreed, but his strict principles and judicious nature often gave him a haughty air. Manesty had seen this "air" in full effect, had watched it halt and drive away many men . . . including the son.

Oh, the disappointment young John brought his father, and the guilt Newton harbored for failing his son. Thus the tenuous bond between them—a bond Manesty struggled to help them maintain.

The door swung open and Newton strode in, his wig and suit impeccable, as usual, even though he'd just ridden two hours in from Aveley. Manesty watched his friend advance through the room, clearly on a mission, pausing for a moment here and there to exchange an essential greeting.

Newton pulled out the chair opposite Manesty and, with a flip of his coattails, settled purposefully into his seat. In mere moments a cup of steaming tea appeared at his elbow, the immediacy of it a testimony that he regularly conducted business here. Newton pushed it to the side and addressed his friend without formal greeting.

"I have received two letters in the space of two weeks from the Guinea Coast." He reached into his greatcoat as Manesty sipped his coffee. "From my son."

Manesty settled his cup in the saucer. "The *Harwich* must be well on her way to the land of opium and silk by now."

"The *Harwich* is. John is not."

Newton opened and placed the letters on the table between them. "One is dated 1745, the other early this year."

Manesty placed his fingertips on the letters, barely glancing at them. "In summary?"

Newton frowned. "He is . . . living among slaves on the Plantains."

"He commands them?"

"He is one of them."

Manesty raised a brow and picked up the top page, scanning the smudged but precise writing. . . . *live in an almost naked state . . . not had half a good meal* . . . He looked up. "How did this come to pass?" He waved away the question. "That matters not. What is your plan of action?"

Newton leaned his arms on the table. "He begs me to use my influence—to arrange a rescue. According to the *List*"—he tapped the section on arrivals and departures—"one ship leaves Liverpool within a week for Sierra Leone."

"The *Greyhound*."

"The very one."

The wheels were already spinning in Manesty's head. His business in London—which meetings could he delay? What tasks could he delegate? He squinted as he mulled over his obligations.

"I've settled Anthony Gother with the crew, and she'll finish taking on supplies any day."

Newton nodded. "I wonder what goods I could offer you in the form of trade." At Manesty's quizzical look, Newton explained. "Once John is found, your captain may have to redeem him."

"Ah. So the question is, What would a European trader require in exchange for a European slave?" He stroked his chin. "A bolt of English cloth, perhaps. Or a brace of fine pistols."

Newton waved his hand. "Whatever the cost, I will pay it."

Manesty considered his friend. Though Newton was often displeased with a son he found shiftless and dependent, he still hung hope on him. In a very deep and complex way, the man loved his boy. He just seemed incapable of properly expressing it.

Newton took a breath to speak, reconsidered, then plunged forward anyway.

"If he is . . . disinclined to leave—that is, if he does not believe I am pleased to send for him . . ." He shook his head at this. "Ask your captain to make mention of a Miss .Catlett of Chatham."

Manesty remained passive, choosing to let the moment play out.

Newton pulled several sheets of paper from another pocket. "He writes to her, declaring his undying love."

Manesty noted his friend's distaste for that particular emotion, evident in both his inflection and posture. He made an offer.

"I meet today with a young Naval officer assigned to the dockyard there, a Captain Alexander Todd. If you wish, I can entrust the letters to him."

Newton shook his head. "I am reluctant to pass them along. I know the girl's mother, and she does not think well of John . . . or me. Not since Elizabeth's death and my remarriage. Not since I took the boy away to sea." He checked the massive wall clock, pocketed the letters, and stood. "I must away."

He held out his hand, and Manesty stood and gripped it in both of his. "If John is to be found, we will find him."

Newton nodded once, opened his mouth to speak, then

closed it. He nodded again, frowning, then turned and marched briskly out the door.

*A conflicted man, John Newton,* Manesty thought, his heart aching. He paid his tab, collected his papers, and followed the same path to the door.

Outside, on Lombard Street, he paused to reorganize his day. The coffeehouse door opened and slammed shut behind him, and a deep voice spoke from his left shoulder.

"It seems we are on the same mission."

Manesty turned to encounter a sizable man in the customary trappings of a London gentleman, but unmistakably military in bearing. His ramrod posture and self-possession gave him away.

"Navy?"

"Marines," he said, indicating they should walk a bit.

Manesty complied, intrigued that a Marine would frequent Lloyd's when the Little Devil was widely considered the military's social club. The Marine wasted no time.

"I, too, am searching for a sailor named John Newton."

Manesty was careful to let no expression show. He could not know the military's intent with John.

"And you are. . . ?"

"Captain Mathias Ward."

"And who has set you on this search?"

"The same lady of whom you just spoke—Miss Catlett."

Manesty tried not to show his surprise at that declaration but felt he probably failed. He needed to tread lightly with this Marine. He needed to think . . . to redirect.

"And what brings you to Lloyd's today, Captain Ward?"

"I find the news there to be more reliable than information

from the Admiralty. And you just proved that conclusion."

Manesty made no reply to that but continued walking, hoping the Marine would give him a piece to the puzzle of John's whereabouts. He was not disappointed.

"The captain's correspondence with the Admiralty shows a midshipman named John Newton deserted the *Harwich* in March of 1745, was flogged and demoted, then released to the English slaver *Levant* in May. That ship completed her mission and returned to England. Without John Newton."

The Marine had rattled off the details like any good soldier.

"The captain died, the crew has disbursed, and the first mate either knows or will reveal nothing. The trail had run cold . . . until today."

Manesty continued his line of questioning. "And what is your relationship to Miss Catlett?"

"She is my apprentice."

"Your . . . apprentice."

"I am a physician. I specialize in herbal remedies." At Manesty's dubious expression, he continued . . . a little forcefully. "It is a worthy therapy for any ailment."

The Marine abruptly came to a halt and waved a hand. "But that is neither here nor there, which I am certain was your intent."

He reached into his pocket and pulled out an envelope.

"You have a ship bound for Sierra Leone. John Newton was last heard from in that area." He thrust the envelope toward Manesty. "I have a letter from Miss Catlett addressed to John Newton—a letter that may compel him to return, should he be located and . . . 'disinclined to leave,' I believe the gentleman said."

Manesty took the envelope, still wary of this imposing man. "Eavesdropping is ungentlemanly in the extreme."

The Marine smiled. "Yes." He leaned forward. "But it has proved valuable too often to completely discredit."

And he stalked away, a confident soldier who had completed a mission.

Manesty stood on Lombard, turning the letter over and over in his hands. Finding a man—even a white man—in an area the size of Ireland, dotted with habitable islands and numerous inlets, was akin to finding an innocent man at Newgate prison. And if the man did not wish to be found, or his African master worked to keep his presence secret, the odds were even worse.

It would take more than an alert captain with a directive and a promising letter, Manesty realized with mounting unease. It would take a miracle.

# CHAPTER

## 7

With a word and a handshake, Newton was spared a slow death.

Gone were the poverty and squalor, the gnawing hunger and maltreatment. An Englishman's suit replaced the shabby shirt and trousers. Boots covered feet still rough from a year of living like a savage in the elements.

Newton could only guess at what had led the trader Clow to make such a generous offer for his life. Perhaps the man was in desperate need of an apprentice. Perhaps he was shocked at seeing a fellow Englishman so poorly treated. They had not discussed it, and it was doubtful they ever would.

But oh . . . what a difference a shave, a sliver of soap, a coat, and proper hat could render. He never could have imagined he'd be so thankful for such common items. And the food—at first, just a little rice and pigeon peas with a cup of broth. But then, within days, ground nuts, maize, and sweet potatoes.

Now, weeks later, he used his knife, with hands that no longer shook, to slice through the string holding closed a banana leaf and breathed in the wonderful aroma of baked fish. He forked a piece of the succulent meat into his mouth, closing his eyes in pure delight.

"Spanish mackerel," Clow said between bites. "Fresh from the boat this morning."

Newton swallowed and speared a piece of nut-covered yam. He still savored every bite of every meal, appreciative of each morsel, unconvinced his good fortune would hold with Pey Ey and her tribe so close at hand.

The five-course meal progressed in European style, Newton sampling a variety of dishes, still wary of the effects of too much food in his shrunken stomach. Between courses Newton regaled Clow with the status of his household finances, to which his employer would nod, saying only, "Good . . . good . . ."

The constant gusting wind of the rainy season blew through the house, dropping the temperature but coating everything with a light sheen of moisture. Newton sipped his tea and caught himself tracing a geometric proof onto the tabletop just as Clow leapt to his feet.

"Ah! McCraig, my good man." He sprang toward the doorway, large hand already outstretched.

Standing there, dripping yet smiling with good cheer, was the man whom Clow liked to call his Kittam "factor." He was nothing like Newton had imagined. As fair and blond as

Newton was dark, McCraig exuded such sophistication and grace that Newton thought him woefully out of place in this part of the world. He tried to imagine what had drawn such a man to the bowels of hell. Had he escaped a heinous crime? Was he the unlucky third son, bereft of an inheritance and letter of introduction? *Intriguing man, Mr. McCraig,* Newton thought and determined right then to unearth the man's story.

Their employer made quick introductions and seated Mc-Craig across the table. Newton took his own seat, covertly watching McCraig fold himself into the high-backed chair and casually cross his legs in a long elegant line. He wondered how this man could be the same ruthless agent Clow had described.

"Gentlemen," Clow said as he topped off their wine, "together you will manage my business interests in Guinea. Newton has a head for numbers, and McCraig—well . . . let us say that you have an exquisite expertise in managing product."

Clow raised his glass and McCraig inclined his head, wordlessly accepting the compliment.

"You will make equal commissions on every trade, every sale, along the Kittam River. And I have every confidence you will disappoint neither me nor each other."

Clow's smile was so open and generous, his prediction so certain, that Newton's heart swelled with long-suppressed confidence.

Clow stood and raised his glass again. "To wealth and glory."

Newton leapt to his feet as McCraig unfolded his long frame and stood in one fluid motion. They raised their glasses to their employer.

"Wealth and glory."

—————

*The Kittam River, Guinea*

McCraig strolled along the packed wooden holding pens under a clear sky, his hands clasped behind his well-tailored back. He looked over the captives, Newton wryly observed, as if he were window-shopping in the Royal Exchange. The raider trailed behind him, talking nonstop, extolling the benefits of the captives, working up to his price.

Newton kept a short distance, making notes in his ever-present logbook. He noted the raider as "a weasel in Englishmen's clothing," trying out various words that might rhyme with "weasel." He had a gift for rhyme—had, in fact, gotten himself into trouble aboard the *Levant* for inventing crude songs about the captain. But his head was buried in the notebook mostly because he was doing anything he could think of to avoid looking, really looking, at the captives.

The bulk of them had arrived last night, yoked and driven like oxen into the black trader's sheds, the whip keeping steady pace beside, behind, and in front of them. Newton had been on hand to see the coffles removed and to record details about the "dry goods" in his logbook.

He'd looked into the captives' faces and saw reflected there everything from panic to defiance to defeat. Some of them cried, slow tears making paths down their dusty cheeks. Others looked at nothing. A few stared at everyone and everything with raw fury. He understood them, for hadn't he been in a similar situation? Hadn't he been tied to the post, a whip at his back? And hadn't he ultimately survived it?

"What is the total, Mr. Newton?" McCraig's smooth voice snapped him back to the task at hand. This was a stall tactic. McCraig knew exactly how much cargo the shallop could hold, but Newton scrutinized his notes and replied with efficiency.

"An acquisition of seven would bring us to full capacity."

"They are a particularly skilled set of captives," the raider pressed. "We liberated them from a village of craftsmen, known for making tools, musical instruments, and such."

McCraig raised a brow. "They appear very strong for musicians."

"Oh, they do not *play* the instruments, just make them."

"Indeed," McCraig rejoined, just shy of sarcasm.

He stopped and squatted to look over a captive child. The boy, tragically cherubic and all of five or six, looked back at him with mournful eyes and quivering lip. The raider noted his buyer's sudden interest.

"Ahh . . . you like this one, yes?"

McCraig's eyes never left the child. "We have no interest in children, as I keep reminding you. And this one is in the first stages of the rubella fever."

The raider's mouth fell open in panic.

McCraig stood. "Undoubtedly the entire shipment is tainted by now." He sighed. "Too bad."

"No, no!" The raider began rushing from pen to pen, gesturing wildly. "They are all very strong! Very healthy!"

Newton eyed a sculpted, well-muscled, and defiant captive who reminded him very much of—He cut that thought to the quick. He would not think of Tome—how the slave had brought him food and water under threat of punishment . . . how he had smuggled the letters onto the merchant ship.

McCraig noticed the object of Newton's interest and faced the captive through the bars. The two men stood at the same height, in the same confident manner, and engaged in a stare-down. Suddenly the captive lifted his chin and spat into Mc-Craig's face. In a flash McCraig's hand shot through the bars, gripped the captive by the throat above the iron collar, and slammed his face into the bars.

The raider sucked in his breath. "I shall have him whipped!"

McCraig kept his grip on the captive's throat, choking him, but the captive refused to break eye contact or react.

McCraig smiled pleasantly. "No. I shall take my pleasure . . . in other ways." He eased his grip on the captive's neck, still smiling, looking over his athletic build appreciatively. He removed a pristine white handkerchief from his breast pocket, wiped the spittle from his face, then wiped his hands.

"Very strong, indeed."

The raider hesitated, then licked his lips. "We have a trade, then?"

McCraig nodded once. "We have a trade."

———

The close of the hour found the terms settled, the slaves quarantined, and the raider packing up his newly acquired flints, knives, and brass pans.

As the village chief insisted his "valued clients" be entertained into the evening, Newton whiled away the afternoon with McCraig under a stand of mighty teak trees, chewing nuts and sipping palm wine in companionable silence. He was a hundred miles from Pey Ey and the Plaintains, he held a highly lucrative position, and somehow in the bargain he'd acquired a new and interesting companion.

He inhaled the heavy scent of the teaks' yellow flowers, letting his gaze roam across the lush, tree-covered hillsides. He listened to the African women's chatter carried on the breeze from their distant hut where they washed and pounded the rice. And he had a revelation: He was free . . . as free as the butterflies landing lightly on the backs of his hands. And he was free in a place where he could appear without disguise. He could do or say anything he liked, be as abandoned as he pleased, with little control. It was a strange and overwhelming relief, and a cause for celebration.

Newton picked up his cup and saluted the river. "To wealth and glory."

McCraig smiled a little. "The very things we were denied in England but afforded in Africa. And why, you may ask?" He cocked his head at Newton with a little smirk. "Because our skin is white. And in this part of the world, a white man holds the power. The white man is God."

Those were the most words Newton's partner had directed toward him in the three days since they'd left Sherbro and sailed up the Kittam. And they were spoken with barely controlled fervor. Intriguing. Newton chewed some nuts, pondering.

"It is a fine day to be white." He sipped his wine, then broached another topic. "Now if we only had women on our laps, this tableau would be complete."

When McCraig finally responded, he was quietly deliberate. "Tonight the chief will offer you a selection of his concubines. You will choose a young beautiful native called Isata."

"Isata," Newton repeated.

"You *must* choose this woman."

"Or the chief will be offended?"

McCraig sipped his wine. "Let us just say, you will not be disappointed."

———

When Newton left his hammock the next morning, he did so with a new perspective on the advantages of coastal trade. Never could he have imagined a night so erotic, so exhausting, so . . . satisfying. The concubine Isata certainly knew how to please a man, and he reviewed many of the ways she had pleased him as he made the short trek to the river.

Two black crewmen, armed with cutlasses and daggers, already stood in McCraig's shallop, guarding the five slaves from a previous trade downriver. The four men were handcuffed and shackled in pairs, positioned at the fore and aft oars, watching the shore with unconcealed curiosity. One woman sat on the floor in the stern.

The seven new acquisitions, their hands tied behind them, their arms pinioned, shuffled toward the river's edge. As each approached, a villager threw buckets of water on him, rinsing off the filth and stench from the holding pens. Then, whilst the captive spat out the river water, another villager cracked a whip to get him moving, always moving.

Newton stood with McCraig, taking it all in, making notes in his book. "These are very strong and healthy men."

McCraig looked at him sharply. "Cargo, my friend. They are

not men; they are cargo. Granting them souls exceeds their worth."

Newton raised an eyebrow. "And the female? What is her worth?"

"What is the worth of a fine Araby steed . . . or a barrel of Spanish rum?"

"That much, eh?"

McCraig smiled. "A fraction of that."

"Oh-ho! I pity the poor woman who defies her father and marries you."

"That would be wasted pity, for I am married."

Newton was struck dumb with that little tidbit. He was not so much surprised at the news but at the lurch of his heart. His singular goal, his only hope in life, was to be united in marriage with Mary. His greatest fear was that she would be bound to a man like McCraig. A sigh of dismay escaped him, and McCraig mistook its meaning.

"Afford her no sympathy. The union is entirely to her advantage—a comfortable existence and an absent husband." He grimaced. "I daresay, it is the very picture of a woman's dream."

A sound like a screeching hawk drew their attention toward a line of mangroves on a gentle rise a hundred yards distant. As they watched, the concubine Isata burst through the tree line and ran toward them, her full and naked breasts instantly rekindling Newton's desire for the young beauty. He thought she might be rushing toward him to bid a final *adieu,* and the idea put a gentle smile on his face . . . until he saw the band of women chasing after her.

"Vandi! Vandi!" Isata screamed as she stumbled down the

sandy rise. Her striped skirt caught on a shrub, throwing her forward and revealing even more of her firm flesh. At the water's edge the defiant captive McCraig had choked in retaliation turned, straining against his captors, shouting her name in return. The whip cracked through the air, the cacophony of sound overwhelming.

Isata regained her feet, all but stripped of clothing, and turned her attention to Newton, holding out her arms in supplication. She cried out in her native tongue, tears streaming down her cheeks, and Newton stood as if glued to the sandy spot, fascinated.

He watched as the band of women wrestled her to the ground, pinning her with their weight, restraining her by sheer number.

Now the defiant captive was shouting at Newton, his face drawn into a frightening mask as he spat out a stream of words.

Newton turned to McCraig. "What is this about?"

"I do not speak the Mende language, you understand." McCraig paused to roll the ash off the tip of his cigar. "But I would imagine that she is begging for mercy, and he is threatening your life."

"*My* life?"

"You did make excellent use of his wife last night."

Newton's mouth settled into a grim line. Animosity crawled up the back of his neck and hovered, growling in his throat even as his lust rose for the wailing, writhing woman.

"His wife."

"Yes. She was under the impression that if she pleased you last night, she would be in the shallop with her husband this morning. Despite his unruly behavior yesterday."

"But that is not the way of it, is it?"

"Of course not. Although I daresay she pleased you, yes?"

Newton reluctantly inclined his head. McCraig puffed lazily on his cigar.

"She was always intended for the village chief. I simply used his hospitality, your desire, and the necessity for punishment in tandem." He sighed. "But I do despise such drama. So . . . unproductive."

Newton was forming a caustic reply when, with a primal scream, the defiant slave broke free from his captors and charged past them toward Isata. The villager wielding the whip let it fly, the first lash cutting across the captive's bound arms and driving him to his knees. He staggered upright, and the second lash caught him on the neck and shoulder. He lurched forward and fell onto his face. As the villager hauled back for the next lash, the whip flew backward out of his hand. Surprised, he looked around.

McCraig stood with one boot on the end of the whip, arms crossed. "I am reimbursed only for cargo delivered alive and in good condition. Do you have the goods to trade for this property?"

The villager opened his mouth to argue but reconsidered and gave the answer he knew he should. "No, sir."

McCraig stared at the villager until the man lowered his gaze. He stepped off the whip. "Carry on." Two men yanked the captive Vandi to his feet and hustled him onto the shallop. The women lifted the sobbing Isata and carried her back toward the village. Newton watched it all in silence, settling his roiling emotions into one hard sentiment.

As the last of the goods were stowed away, Newton joined McCraig at the water's edge, turning his back to the boat.

"We are collaborators in this business, so we must agree to . . . abide each other." Newton leaned forward. "But you will not use me in your little games again."

"Or. . . ?"

"Or I will strike at you in kind."

McCraig raised a mocking brow and clipped off the foot of his cold cigar. "I will remind you that we are trading slaves— black gold, I think they are calling it now—on a barbaric coast." He stashed the cigar in his pocket and looked his partner dead in the eye. "Everybody uses everybody."

McCraig walked to the gangway, climbed into the shallop, and reclined under the cloth canopy.

Newton hesitated on the bank, looking toward the now-quiet mangroves. He considered his situation. This was a troublesome business—brutal, calculating, and yes, lucrative. It filled him with conflicting emotions, and he wasn't sure how to manage them. Well. He would make his fortune on this barbaric coast, but he would do it quickly. And then he would find a way back to London, to civilization . . . before he became a savage himself.

# CHAPTER

# 8

*The Sewa River, Northern Sherbro*
*Early January 1747*

Newton swept through the door of the Big House, handing his hat to the servant girl, appearing to take no notice but covertly assessing her. She might be one of several women offered him later tonight.

He masked his interest by brushing the fine dust from his coat and gazing around the interior. As African houses went, this was a sizable bungalow—rooms open to the dry Sahara winds, the mud walls pitiable by English standards but fitting for this culture. As his arrival at the Big House had been anticipated the moment his boot touched the shoreline, the bartering space was primed—the drinking table situated between three hammocks, three tumblers of European design at the ready.

He sighed inwardly. This was the part of trading he liked the least. Never much of a tippler, he resented the required sampling of rum even before they visited the slave barracoons or uttered a word of negotiation. His partner saw it as a necessary cog in the wheel of the circuit trade.

As McCraig explained it, they plied the village chiefs and traders with quality rum, the well-oiled men gave up their best captives, a good portion of the captives were sold to the Sugar Islands, the raw molasses they harvested sailed up to the Newport distilleries, the rum from the molasses came directly back to Africa, and the process started all over again. The perfection of world commerce, McCraig called it.

The chiefs understood the value of "clients" like Newton, and they treated him well. He was welcomed into their villages, feted with choice food, entertained with tribal dances, and offered his pick from the chiefs' concubines. In exchange, Newton would bring out his best British goods.

This particular chief, however, could be trouble. Newton had unknowingly bedded one of his wives—his first wife, in fact—last month at a village downriver during a festival to the new moon. Dressed in their bird feathers and adorned with charms, their bodies painted yellow and red, the men and women danced and dined through the moon's rising, calling on the spirits of their ancestors. In the midst of the celebration, an older woman approached, dancing for him, offering herself to him. And he had, naturally, accepted. These passionate, wanton creatures were so different from the chaste Englishwomen with their modesty and morals. It was intoxicating, and Newton reveled in it . . . even if it labeled him a libertine.

Fortunately, this chief needed him and his access to firearms.

The Sulima warlords were gaining power in the north and making their way south, attacking neighboring villages for supremacy. The chief would defend his village the British way, and he would forgive Newton's dalliance with his wife. For now.

The chief entered from a back room. Like most Mende men, he was built like a bull—slabs of fat and muscle bunched around his torso, narrow hips and lean legs poking out from a blue-and-white striped sarong. His painted face and tall embellished hat only enhanced his fierceness. The row of wooden sticks hanging like a *lavallière* from his thick neck slapped against his chest as he stalked across the packed earthen floor toward Newton.

He stopped two feet away, and the two men regarded each other warily. Custom dictated that the chief open each exchange, but he remained silent as his black eyes bored into his guest.

Newton returned the stare, relaxing his stance, reminding himself that the Mende people were farmers, not vicious warriors. They attacked only when provoked.

The chief's eyes cut to a point across Newton's left shoulder, and the moment was interrupted by the timely arrival of the village broker.

"Newton!" the man called out in his accented English. He burst through the door, bowed to the chief, and placed his hand on Newton's shoulder, seemingly nonplussed by his leader's dark look. They stood in silence for another long moment until the chief made a brief statement in his own tongue and turned toward the hammocks. The broker did not translate, but his hand urged Newton forward.

They relaxed around the table, Newton pulling a decanter of

rum from his satchel, the broker pouring generous amounts into each glass with the traditional opening prayer of "Ngewo willing." As they settled into their hammocks to sip the fine liquor, the parade of women began. This one offering them dried figs, tall, elegant, and small-breasted with multiple rings around her neck, signifying beauty. Another one delivering kola, her large breasts swinging as, like the temptress Eve, she offered Newton the apple-like fruit. He bit into it, surprised at the flavor of green coffee. Then came a very young girl, shy and childlike, with her offer of deep crimson plums. Nuts, fish, and spiced rice came to the men balanced on the heads and in the hands of the dark-skinned women, each one clad in matching skirt and headdress, their bosoms proudly displayed beneath colorful rings and necklaces of boars' teeth.

Newton did not need the rum's intoxicating powers to stimulate his interest in the negotiations. The blood pumped hot and thick through his veins. He could hardly wait to hand over his goods and return for the evening's festivities.

The chief barked out a brief sentence, and the broker translated.

"Dee chief say his wife, she not be well. She not be in service tonight."

Newton looked at the broker. "Please tell your chief I am sorry to hear of his wife's illness."

The broker translated and the chief shot Newton a dark look that said, "I am sure that you are." He stood abruptly and the other men followed suit, traipsing behind him out of the house and across the village center to the holding pens.

Newton shook the lingering desire from his mind, focusing

on the task before him. This was his first and northernmost stop along the Sewa. Both he and the broker would attempt to take advantage of the other's largess as they bartered slaves for common goods. He would select no more than four prime specimens and give up no more than four guns each. The baft, pans, and flints would sweeten the deal. The knives were negotiable.

They approached the barracoons, and Newton heard the captives before he saw them. Their mournful song drifted with the clouds of fine dust through the palms, the melody haunting and beautiful. He knew from past translations that they sang primarily of their tribal history, weaving in their present sorrow and wretched circumstances. He also knew that many of them were suspected criminals—murderers, thieves, and adulterers spared execution by questionable evidence. Indeed, he would not be surprised to find the chief's wife among them.

For centuries Africans had rid their villages of troublemakers by selling them up or down the river. Now they were able to purge the continent of such menace by trading them across an ocean. But Newton also suspected that a greater number were captured by treachery and force—wives torn from husbands, children torn from mothers. He suspected this but felt no compulsion to change it. His was purely a business transaction.

The broker brought out the males first, in pairs, handcuffed to each other, their legs shackled, their necks circled with iron collars. He commanded them to jump about, demonstrating the condition of every limb. Then he yanked on their collars to bare their teeth. Newton had the broker separate out the best specimens, then whittled down the number to four.

And then the real negotiations began. As Newton suspected,

the chief was most interested in firearms. They stood together, arms crossed, and bartered through the broker until both parties were satisfied. At a nod from the chief, the slaves were sent to Newton's shallop, attended by the armed guards, and the British goods were brought to shore.

The entire process took less than an hour, but the intense haggling under a blazing sun made it feel more like three. Newton stood at the river's edge, hot, thirsty, and ready to be entertained. At the chief's signal they headed back to the village.

As they marched past the fields lying thirsty and fallow in the dry season, Newton congratulated himself on the transaction. Several more stops like this along the Sewa would net him enough dry goods to relax along the coastline for weeks . . . perhaps acquire another concubine.

The chief's sudden exclamation and surge forward interrupted Newton's designs. He looked and found at once the cause of the man's delight.

In the doorway of the Big House stood a young and exquisitely beautiful woman. Clad head to toe in a yellow sarong of raw silk, one delicate shoulder exposed, and multiple gold rings around her neck, Newton found her strangely demure and exotic, a blend of the best of English and African femininity. She had eyes only for the chief, taking his arm, smiling tenderly into his painted face.

Newton knew in an instant he would not be offered this woman tonight. Yet he would do his best to have her . . . perhaps on his next visit.

The chief cupped the woman's face, murmuring to her, making her blush, deepening her smile. He turned slightly to the broker and rattled off a sentence.

"Dee chief say, dis be dee chief's daughter, Onya."

Newton raised a brow at that revelation, bowed, and smiled a greeting.

"My pleasure . . . Onya."

"She be here from Romarong, at dee mouth of dee great river."

The broker turned to Onya and said in English, "Dis be dee Englishman, John Newton."

At the mention of his name, her smile faltered.

The chief nodded toward a line of mangroves at a short distance, spitting out an order and stalking into the house with his daughter once it was pronounced. The broker bowed after him, then turned to Newton.

"Dee chief say you may retire to dee hammock within dee trees dere, and you will be served refreshment."

Newton nodded and sauntered toward the trees, reflecting on the lovely Onya. He relaxed into the hammock, his hands linked behind his head, tossing about possibilities of drawing her out until he drifted into a light doze.

The sun was still high in the cloudless sky when he awoke, refreshed, and looked around him. Seated on a stool under a nearby pepper tree was the very object of his desire. He shifted in the hammock to draw her attention.

She looked over at him, eased to her feet, and approached him with a smile and a crystal glass.

"Wine, Mr. Newton?"

He took the heavy glass from her, admiring her long delicate fingers. He watched her uncover a small table near his feet. She selected a bowl and passed it to him.

"The peanuts are fresh." She looked back to the table. "And I can offer you kola and peaches."

He cracked open a peanut shell. "Your English is very good." And it was. Her accent was decidedly European, but neither British nor Spanish nor Portuguese. It was none of them and all of them.

"I have a tutor—a Jesuit who refuses to abandon Romarong to the Mohammedans and pagans."

He arched a brow. "Pagans?" He tossed the peanuts into his mouth. "You are a Mende—most certainly what a Jesuit would call a pagan."

She smiled. "I was once. Now I am a Christian."

Newton choked on the half-chewed peanuts. He sat up quickly, nearly throwing himself out of the hammock, and coughed whilst Onya pounded his back. He gulped the palm wine, and his throat cleared. He breathed normally a few times, then tested his voice.

"Christian!"

"Yes."

"I can scarcely believe a Mende chief would allow his daughter to worship any god other than Ngewo."

She shrugged. "My father is a very forward-thinking man. It is why he sent me to the Mountain . . . to the Jesuits. He honors the Mende gods of his ancestors but is intrigued by the Christian God."

"Whatever for?"

Newton was just as astonished as he sounded. In his way of thinking, the Christian religion and all of its trappings were sim-

ply a means of escaping hell. There was no joy in it—no dancing, no feasting, no communing with nature. It was flat, regi-
mented, constricting.

Onya retrieved her stool and sat, putting the small table
between them.

"The living God captivates his heart and mind. The Mendes
must consult the spirits of their ancestors—the dead, dwelling in
the waters of the great rivers."

Newton jutted his chin at her as he cracked the peanut shells.

"And yet, as a *Christian*, you defy your faith and wear the
Mende rings on your neck—the rings on the water's surface . . .
the water of your *ngafa*."

She touched the gold rings and conceded the point.

"I wear them in honor of my mother. But they mean nothing to me."

"As Christianity means nothing to me."

It was casually stated, and it would have cut his mother to
the quick to hear it. But he spoke true. Like his father, he had
given up that cold faith years ago and never looked back.

Onya gave him an intense look. "Has no one told you of the
living God?"

Newton waved a hand dismissively. "Oh, I was weaned on
the fables—the catechism, Bennet's *Oratory*, Defoe's *Instructor*,
the poems of Watts. It is all, as a sailor once claimed, 'enduring
superstition.'" He sipped his wine. "I much prefer the logic of
Cicero, Virgil, Euclid."

"So you cannot imagine a life lived as the Jesuits recommend—in imitation of Christ?"

Newton snorted. "Who would want to imitate Christ?

Womanless, homeless, at the end—friendless, dead at thirty-three."

"And yet, a thousand years later, you know him by name." Onya leaned forward on her stool. "A thousand years from now, who will remember a womanizer, a destroyer of families and homes, a slave trader on the coast of Africa? Who will remember *your* name, John Newton?"

He sprang out of the hammock and advanced on her, kicking over the table and stool she'd hastily vacated, backing her up against the pepper tree. He placed his hands against the bark at the sides of her head.

"Men are complex and powerful creatures, my sweet." He took his time looking over her high cheekbones and full lips. "But you are far too beautiful to attempt to understand them. Like your mother, you should simply try to please them."

Onya stood her ground against the tree.

"Unlike my mother, sir, I am very well educated in the complexities of men. And I am far less likely to expose my family to any man bent on destruction."

Newton stood so close to her that he nearly pinned her against the tree. "Truly?"

He trailed his finger down the side of her face and throat until his hand settled near the top of her sarong. Onya looked him dead in the eye, showing neither fear nor concern. He sighed.

"If you are sincerely interested in understanding men, perhaps we could retire into these mangroves and discover together what you will and will not . . . expose."

Onya's lips flattened into a thin smile. "I think not. My

father needs you and your firearms . . . for now. But I neither need nor desire anything from you."

Newton traced a pattern across Onya's caramel skin until she struggled to breathe, her chest rising and falling dramatically. Her face continued to show nothing but bland interest.

"Brave words you speak, my fragile Onya. But make no mistake—I always get what I want."

Newton broke contact, retrieving his glass and sipping his palm wine as he settled back into the hammock.

Onya put a steady hand to her chest. "You are incorrigible." And she turned her back on him, walking regally toward the house.

Newton laughed. *Incorrigible*. The Jesuits had taught her well.

She stopped a few yards away and turned, tilting her head, a sad smile enhancing her beauty.

"I will pray for you, John Newton."

He smirked and threw the Mende creator-god back at her. "Ngewo take care of you."

He watched with satisfaction as her smile faded.

"And God be with you."

He stared hard at her retreating back, mentally throwing at her every blasphemous and profane thought he could muster. A beautiful woman and her simpleminded faith were no match for his depravity. He was Circe. He was the African's Narcissus. He was Sodom and Gomorrah.

He smiled and reached for the peanuts, cracking their shells in the same way he'd splintered Onya's Jesuit-trained poise. She had made a worthy attempt at saving his soul. But he loved sin and would not forsake it.

# CHAPTER

## 9

*Chatham, Kent*
*Mid January 1747*

Another Christmas. Another New Year. Another morning at the window, waiting for Jack to climb into the coach that would carry him down Chatham's snow-covered streets, across London, and north to Bedford School.

Mary leaned her forehead against the frosty glass and fought back the waves of despair that almost daily washed over her now. Another year had passed—a spring of anticipation and adventure . . . a summer of hopes built and dashed. At Michaelmas, during the harvest feast of well-fattened goose and huge slices of bread, she'd looked around the dinner table at her animated brother and his captive audience, at the Marine and her parents, and it struck her that winter was coming—the days shorter, the nights longer, the gardens lifeless and austere.

And just like that, she was back at the window, eighteen years old and no closer to an answer than she'd ever been . . . no closer to understanding the tenuous, invisible thread that bound her heart to a childhood friend, now a man she barely knew.

She closed her eyes and relaxed her grip on the book in her lap. It was her constant companion of late. She was embarrassed to admit that the words on its pages had been a somewhat last resort for her crumbling spirit. When her beloved operas and plays and novels had provided no answers, she'd wandered into the back parlor and spied her mother's Bible on the mahogany occasional table next to the chaise lounge. The supple leather book seemed to call to her, and she'd walked over, moved the spectacles off the cover, and opened it.

That brisk November day, she'd begun scouring the Testaments, searching for words of hope and peace. She studied for hours, frustrated, not so much by the sixteenth-century prose— she was an avid reader of Shakespeare—but by the complex implications. She stunned her mother by requesting instruction with the vicar of St. Bartholomew's Chapel. Two days a week she huddled in the stone oval, the sun slanting feebly through the narrow Gothic windows, listening as the vicar read her the Scriptures where time and again people petitioned the Lord and did not give up. The persistent widow in Luke. Jesus in the Garden. And finally, Hannah.

It was Hannah's cry of "remember me" that unleashed the weeping. Mary poured out her heart in the chapel, in the parlor, in the attic room. In the same bitterness of soul she prayed— *Where is John Newton, Lord? Is he alive? Just give me an answer—yes or no. How long must I ask? Yes or no, Lord?*

*Please . . . answer me. Or take this longing from my heart . . .*

And just like the barren Hannah, she was met with silence . . . week after week of silence. Food lost its flavor. The holidays lost their sparkle. Not even Jack could shake her from the relentless sadness. It was, she supposed, her time of barrenness—empty, deserted, lonely.

But unlike Hannah, she did not have a high priest—she did not have an Eli who would say, "The God of Israel grant thee thy petition."

So she sat at the window, watching the snow fall, asking the same question over and over again—*How long, Lord . . .*

———

*Turner's Peninsula*
*Late January*

Newton stood at the highest point on the neck of land, easily locating *Stella Polaris* in the rainless, star-studded sky. He turned his body due north, just as he had done countless times this month, looked across the Kittam River to the Guinea mountains, imagined Madrid and her *Palacio Real*, Normandy and her sheer limestone cliffs, and swept across the Mediterranean Sea to England.

This was his final climb to the point. He stood among the baobab and corkwood, listened to the owl hoot and the frogs croak, and was filled with neither sorrow nor regret. At the age of twenty-two, he had finally found a place and position that rewarded him for his efforts. Gone was his burning desire to return to his homeland—to a place and people constantly dis-appointed in him.

On the African coast he was successful and powerful. He had his own hut with household servants and two concubines ready to meet his every carnal need. When he returned from one of his regular slave-trading expeditions, he could relax beneath the frankincense tree, fish for bunga in the river, or walk along the beach with his Euclid. No Navy captains harangued him. No religious dogma restrained him.

He lived exactly as he pleased.

True, it was not the life he had envisioned for so long. It did not include the brilliantly lit shops of Cheapside and the gentle-men's clubs at Pall Mall. It did not include Mary.

Sometime in the past weeks he had finally accepted that reality . . . it was why he'd come tonight to face the North Star—that symbol of constancy and faithfulness—for the last time.

He ran the memories through his mind—their first meeting, Christmas in '42, when she was a spirited girl not quite fourteen and he an awestruck boy three years her senior . . . the next Christmas when he returned to Chatham to watch her flit about the rooms, making everyone comfortable with hot drinks and pillows whilst Jack had them all in stitches . . . then the New Year of '45 when he remained mute in her presence, overcome with her effect on him.

Five years . . . three visits . . . hundreds of undeclared wishes.

But war and distance and society had intervened. He would always love her but could not return to her—he had nothing to offer. And her disappointment was so much easier to bear more than three thousand miles away.

Newton stared down *Polaris*. His mission now was on an African coast, with the African people, and he submitted to it. He would embrace the Mende language and culture—sit on their councils and venerate the moon. But he would never marry. Only one woman had ever achieved that level of respect, and he would remain forever loyal to her.

It was, perhaps, fortunate that his mother was gone. He knew of her dream to unite the families—his father had told him of it in the same displeased tones he applied to her love of "religion." It struck Newton that, no matter his early training, he'd followed his father's precedent after all. The Mende practices were far removed from the English and his mother's religion. "Diabolical . . . wretched," she would have called them. Well, then. He supposed he would live and die a wretch among them.

He thrust out his chin to counteract the sudden lurch of his treacherous heart. *Carpe diem,* he told himself as the mosquitoes buzzed and the trees swayed with gusts of bone-dry wind. *Carpe diem.*

# PART II

And there stalks Discord
delighted with her torn mantle.

— VIRGIL

# CHAPTER

## 10

*Chatham, Kent*
*February 1747*

Mary picked up the bottle of pure grain alcohol and considered it. It lacked flavor, color, and odor, but its effects were tremendous. She began to pour.

The liquid passed over the lip and down through the neck, causing an almost immediate reaction. She kept pouring, cupping one hand over the mouth like a funnel until it was nearly full. Carefully, she pushed a cork through the top, sighed, and took a sip of the concoction steeping to her left.

It was marigold night in the Marine's kitchen.

The tincture of marigold blossoms and alcohol was already turning a rich honey color made even more vivid by the cheerful fire crackling in the massive hearth. She carried the jar to a far cupboard where it would sit in darkness for a day or so, the alcohol extracting the essential oil from the blossoms, and then be doled out to soldiers for a variety of stomach ills.

She returned to her perch and picked up the cherrywood pestle to grind the dried leaves in the mortar bowl. These she would mix with a salve to cure a recent outbreak of foot fungus at the dockyard. Itching, burning, peeling, cracking feet were slowing down construction on the *Somerset*—and that simply would not do on Captain Ward's watch.

The Marine had been in his usual bossy mood when Mary and her father had blown with the snow through the kitchen door—late, because Mary had insisted on finding and clipping every mature blossom among the forced marigolds in her hothouse. The man had scowled at her and ushered her father into the parlor, leaving her to unpack her supplies.

On his return he'd barked out his orders for the tincture and salve, lecturing her on the healing powers of the *Calendula*, all the while moving about the kitchen, slamming doors. Then all was silent and a cup of steeping marigold leaves slid under her nose.

"Soulager le coeur," he whispered. *To lighten the heart.*

She sipped the infusion as she ground the leaves. The Marine was an intriguing man. He was gruff and demanding and used the worst sort of language, but he was perceptive and honorable.

On her first visit to his kitchen, he'd shown her the wonders of the black poplar buds, then sent her home with instructions to write three identical letters to John Newton. On her second visit he'd collected the letters without a word, then launched into the wonders of ginseng. By June the letters were taking different routes across the Atlantic, she was mastering the art of powdering slippery elm, and her spirits were buoyed by activity. Summer brought lessons in chamomile and spearmint. Fall brought lavender and silence.

She still came to this kitchen every week, learning about the healing powers of herbs, honoring her promise. But her heart was not in it. Her heart was somewhere in the Atlantic.

The kitchen door banged open, and her heart lurched into her throat as a massive dog burst into the room, standing stock-still, staring at her. It was the largest mastiff she'd ever seen, its shoulders even with hers as she sat paralyzed, watching it drip melting snow on the floor. She knew instinctively she'd never be able to outrun or outmaneuver the beast. And she didn't dare call out. She reached ever so slowly for the knife six inches away, the dog's eyes following her hand, a low growl starting in its throat.

"Samson!"

The dog's head jerked around at the sound and Mary surged up, snatching the knife, holding it in the pinch grip as Jack had instructed her so many times, knees bent, weight on the ball of her right foot, arm swinging back for the throw.

Just then a man filled the doorway, and she pivoted slightly, the knife slicing through the air, piercing the doorframe with a solid *thud*. Mary, the man, and the dog all stared at the knife quivering waist-high in the wood, the man finally looking at her under the low brim of his Denmark.

"You must be Ward's apprentice."

Mary stood there, speechless.

"He said you had remarkably steady aim."

She tried to force her tongue off the roof of her mouth, but it seemed fused there.

The man stepped all the way in, closing the door behind him. He pulled the knife free, depositing it and a wooden crate onto the table. The dog dropped to its haunches with a flick of its master's hand.

He removed his hat, revealing close-cropped black hair and a dark stubble that Mary presumed always shadowed his face. A smile started and grew until it went all the way from his bow-shaped mouth to his holly green eyes.

"I believe the knife saved us the trial of formalities. I am Captain Todd of the Royal Navy, and you must be Miss Catlett."

Mary nodded, trying hard not to stare. She had just thrown a knife and narrowly missed the most beautiful man she had ever seen. He was tall and dark and gracious, and seemed to step right off the pages of one of the novels she so loved to read. She was instantly aware of her own dusty hands and stained apron and the fact that she had not touched her hair since knotting it into a *coiffure* that morning. She could feel long red strands of it hanging around her face and resisted the urge to smooth them behind her ears.

He moved to discard his gloves and coat, then stopped, arching a brow in her direction. "May I?"

"Of course."

She was surprised at how normal she sounded as she stood like a planted tree, watching him remove his brown frock and brush the snow from the turned-down collar and short coattails. He was dressed in working-class style—plain linen shirt and buckskin breeches tucked into boots. His only ornamentation was a linen cravat, which he promptly pulled from his neck and snapped in the air, flinging bits of snow and moisture across the floor. He laid it across the counter, then turned and approached the table, gesturing.

"Shall we sit a moment?"

Mary found her seat as the captain straddled the opposite bench, slapping his thigh. The dog approached, all lagging tongue and sad, adoring eyes, but looking no less fierce. The captain rubbed the loose skin under the massive head, smiling at Mary.

"This is Samson. My apologies you were not properly introduced—he appears rather fierce but is really quite gentle."

Mary sincerely doubted that but knew better than to quibble with a gentleman about his dog. She ran a quick eye over the mastiff sitting obediently at his master's feet, the powerful shoulders even with the table's edge. His coat was a mix of brown and cream . . . rather like a marble cake. She tried for a conversational tone.

"His coat is an interesting color."

"We call it 'brindle'—just an extravagant name for spotted, I think."

She smiled at the captain, caught up in his good humor and grace. The moment stretched as she held his gaze, marveling at such an open countenance on a face so perfectly assembled—from the darkly arched brows, down the Roman nose, to the cleft chin. The impossible symmetry was compelling and unsettling at the same time. She dragged her eyes back to the table, plucked a dried flower from the stash, and began to separate the petals for crushing.

After a few moments of steady work, she watched his hand select a flower, twirling it between long and well-manicured fingers.

"'The sun-observing marigold,'" he quoted.

Her mouth twitched as she reached for another. "A Navy captain who can quote Francis Quarles is a rare find."

The captain chuckled and Mary countered with her own poetic quote.

"'When with serious musing I behold; The graceful and obsequious marigold.'"

The captain sighed. "I suppose for anyone other than George Wither, a word such as 'obsequious' would seem rather . . . pretentious."

Mary bit her lip to halt the grin threatening her hard-won poise. She leisurely plucked the flowers' petals, only a little startled when the captain snapped his fingers and leaned forward.

"'The marigold, that goes to bed with the sun; And with him rises weeping.'"

Mary shook her head in theatric pity. "Poor Perdita—at the mercy of Shakespeare's tragic pen."

The captain groaned and Mary thought hard. He'd stolen her next quote, of course. She ran through lines of seventeenth-century poetry, teasing out a verse that tickled her memory until with a note of triumph, she quoted, "'No marigolds yet closed are; No shadows great appeare.'"

The silence was so long and absolute, Mary looked up from her work to see the captain rubbing his bristled jawline, squinting at the ceiling. With a sigh of exasperation, he caught her eye.

"Might I have a bit of context?"

She smiled beatifically. "I think not."

He grimaced and drummed the table, staring into the fire over her shoulder. After several minutes of continuous drumming, he threw up his hands.

"All right. I yield."

She grinned and decided to stretch the game. "He was a cavalier poet."

"Hmm." The hand went back to the jaw. "Well, that narrows the possibilities to a solid five."

With his gaze redirected to the ceiling, Mary had an opportunity to better observe him. He did not fit the standard image of a Navy man—officer or no. Chatham was a town in which every third house was a beer house and every third man was a soldier, or so the axiom went. And with her father's position as customs officer, she had plenty of interaction with the king's men.

This man had a natural grace and manners sadly lacking at the dockyard. Though dressed as a commoner, his shirt was spotless and of very fine weave. He had an evident curiosity and information beyond his profession, quoting poetry and prose with eloquent ease. His accent was British gentry, and his taste in canine companionship was expensive.

Mary determined there was much more to Captain Todd than a soldier and his dog.

He turned to her and raised a brow. "Lovelace?"

"You are guessing."

"Clearly."

The Marine chose that moment to bang through the adjoining door, interrupting the cozy *tête-à-tête*. He stopped beside the worktable, looking from his unannounced guest to Mary.

"I see you've met the viscount."

Mary stared down at her marigolds, mortified. *Viscount?* This charming, unassuming man was a *viscount?* She felt the heat of a blush creep up her neck and ring in her ears. In one short evening she'd managed to throw a knife at and engage in off-hand sparring with a nobleman. *This* was why one waited for a formal introduction. *This* was why—That thought was interrupted by another. If tonight's social blunder reached her mother's ears . . .

She crushed the dried petals with enough industry to powder them.

The viscount sighed heavily. "I do so despise that title."

The Marine snorted, then leaned down and pounded the dog in the way large men show affection to large animals.

"Well, the earl will be thrilled to hear that."

She felt the Marine approach the table. She didn't look up. She would not look up. The long-forgotten crate scraped across the surface, followed by the tinkling of glass and the Marine's brusque voice.

"What have we here?"

Out of the corner of her eye, she watched the Marine lift every jar from the crate, holding it up to the firelight. Meanwhile, the viscount proceeded to flip the knife end to end on the table—tip, handle, tip, handle. She thought she would scream. Why couldn't they just go away and let her suffer her mortification in silence?

"Precisely the jars we need for the tinctures. Good work, man."

The Marine hauled the crate off the table and carried it away.

Mary shot a fleeting glance at the viscount and was trapped by curious green eyes. She dragged her gaze to the knife, and he halted the movement in midflip, gently settling the blade on the table and leaning toward her.

"Miss Catlett—"

"Now, then . . ." The Marine stomped back through the room and slapped the viscount on the shoulder. "We shall have a glass of port by the parlor fire. By the devil, it's cold out there tonight."

As usual, the Marine did not wait to see that his directive was agreed to, much less followed. He walked to the adjoining door and simply held it open for his guest.

Both Mary and the viscount stood.

"Good evening, Miss Catlett."

"Good evening, Lord . . . Lord . . ." She blinked as she realized the man's full title had not been given her.

"Captain Todd will be fine."

"Captain Todd," she repeated with a tilt of her head.

The captain snapped his fingers, and the mastiff came alongside him, positioning its mammoth head under the waiting hand.

The door closed and the kitchen was quiet again. *Too quiet,* Mary thought, staring at the empty space across the table.

Moments later the door opened to reveal black hair and green eyes. "The answer is Herrick. Robert Herrick. Yes?"

She nodded and he grinned.

"The cavalier poet, indeed. So I will leave you with this: 'Endure the present, and watch for better things.'"

She knew that one: Virgil. She smiled at the closing door, reflecting on the evening and the quote, and suddenly remembering why she knew it. It had been related to her in a letter. From John Newton.

The pain settled around her like a heavy cloak, the light-hearted bantering stifled in its folds. She picked up the pestle with a leaden hand, thinking again of the man so far from here, asking the same questions as she crushed the herb's yellow petals.

She would endure the present. But, oh . . . the persistence of memory. It was a blessing and a curse.

# CHAPTER

## 11

*Turner's Peninsula*
*February 1747*

The cannon-shot reverberated across the cape, jolting Newton from his late-morning catnap as he fished along the Kittam. He reeled in his line, shaking off his lethargy, and climbed the sandy embankment. Just over a distant hill to the west the fumes from McCraig's beach fire lingered, and somewhere nearby, anchored in the Atlantic, was a ship, with a smoking cannon, ready to make a trade.

Newton yawned and stretched. They'd delayed their next expedition, hoping for just such an opportunity to acquire more goods to trade for slaves upriver. He stashed his fishing rod and set out for the beach, considering the awkward timing of the exchange. If the trade went well, McCraig would want to leave on the morrow, and Newton had a duel with an Englishman at dawn, three days hence.

He trekked through the mile of palms and brushwood, his ire rising all over again. The Englishman had mocked him, had accused him of "growing black"—which he, admittedly, had. It was not so much the accusation as the contempt with which the man said it, his beefy frame a handy weapon, no doubt, in past verbal conflicts. Newton vowed to wipe the sneer from his pocked face. And since he couldn't match the man with pure brawn, he'd do it with a pistol. Even turned to the side, his body would be hard to miss at twelve paces.

Newton stomped through the mangroves lining the beach in time to see McCraig climb aboard the vessel anchored offshore to the south. The shells crunched under his feet as he marched toward the smoky fire, the wind blowing past him to send sparks skittering out to sea.

He stared out at the two-masted brigantine, his practiced eye taking in the jolly boat suspended from the stern and the galleries below the quarterdeck. She bobbed in the shallow shore, her sails unbent and flapping in a wind quite fair for speed, the Union Jack flying from the bowsprit. She was English, then. Newton smiled. He much preferred trading with his own countrymen—he understood their logic and the value of their products.

He was scanning the beach for easy firewood when he spotted McCraig, hardly up the ship's side, climbing back over the rail and descending into the canoe, followed step for step by another man. He watched the men paddle steadily toward shore, making quick work of the current, then waded out to grab the mooring rope and pull the boat onto the sand.

A tall rawboned man leapt over the side and splashed through the water, dragging the boat with him. If the short trousers, checked shirt, and knotted handkerchief were not enough to peg him a career seaman, the rolling gait and chaw of tobacco would have to seal it.

He spat into the water and studied Newton with intelligent green eyes.

"John Newton?"

"I am."

The man held out his hand. "Anthony Gother, cap'n of the *Greyhound*, recen'ly a Liverpool."

Newton shook the captain's hand, pegging his rhythmic dialect as distinctly west England, most likely Bristol—his name coming out as "Anfony Gofer." He stood there, watching the captain's eyes rove over his island garb of open white shirt and striped sarong. He raised an eyebrow at McCraig, who was expressionless and silent, as usual. The moment stretched and Newton chose to end it.

"What brings you to Sierra Leone, Captain?"

Gother hesitated. "Ahm . . . the usual—gawld, iv'ry, dyer's wood, beeswax."

"Camwood we have aplenty, but no ivory or beeswax, and the natives melt down any gold they acquire for ornaments. But I expect McCraig already told you this."

" 'Ee did." Gother nodded, then cleared his throat and spat again.

McCraig moved a discreet distance down the beach, and Newton stared after him, annoyed that his partner would leave him in this awkward situation. He returned his gaze to the captain, crossing his arms over his chest, deciding to wait him out.

"The truf be, sir . . ." Gother frowned. "We dropped anchor all 'long the Guinea coast—the estu'ry ta the norf, the Bananawls, now 'ere—looken fer *you*."

Newton nearly panicked at those words. The hair on his tanned arms bristled as he imagined Pey Ey sending for him, anxious to continue her torture. Or the Navy, needing sailors, reneging on their trade as King George's War raged on. How did they find him? He and McCraig would have to depart immediately. The shallop was packed. He would leave McCraig and continue far inland. A man—even an Englishman—could hide forever in the northeast mountains along the Niger. He would—

"Mr. Manesty made me swear ta 'eaven I'd deliver the message ta you pacifically."

Newton shook his head. "Manesty?"

"Joseph Manesty, the Liverpool merchant. The *Greyhound* 'tis part a Manesty's fleet."

Newton blinked. Joseph Manesty. A kind and tender man who was like a father to him . . . or like what a father *should* be, he imagined. And then his blood ran cold with the thought—something terrible, something catastrophic, must have happened to send a ship looking for him. How long had this ship been at sea? Six . . . seven months? It would be too late now!

Newton searched the captain's weathered face, clamping his arms against his sides to avoid shaking the news from the man.

"The message?"

"Come 'ome. 'Ee begs you ta come 'ome."

Newton stared at the man, then burst into laughter, partly with relief and partly with the absurdity of the situation.

Gother looked on with growing alarm. "I've orders ta . . . redeem you from yer master." And he nodded toward McCraig. "Even if it cost 'alf me cargo."

Newton wiped his eyes, continuing to chuckle. "McCraig is not my master. He is my business partner." He grasped Gother's shoulder. "Come, my good man. Let us retire to my village. McCraig will ready your camwood, and I will show you precisely why I will not be going home."

Newton led the captain up the beach and into the mangroves, chatting happily about the responsibilities of being a slave "factor"—the bartering, the trips inland, the high profit.

Gother traipsed along beside him, chewing his tobacco, his long legs matching stride for stride. At the edge of the village, he lurched ahead and turned, halting Newton's progress.

"Then . . . yewl not be a slave yerself?"

Newton snorted at that.

"Praps yer father misread yer notes, then?"

Newton wanted to slap his forehead as he finally grasped the captain's confusion. The letters. At least one of them must have survived the journey to London. His father had asked for Manesty's help, and a rescuer was sent. He smiled and indicated they should walk on.

"I sent them a while back. My situation then was somewhat . . . desperate. But no longer."

Newton led the way to a pair of hammocks beside a small hut. He settled into one and stared up at the captain, who eyed the hammocks with disdain.

"You assant got yerself English chairs, eh?"

Newton grinned. "Not on an island."

Gother sank into his hammock with a sigh but sat up a little straighter when Newton's concubines approached with wooden bowls of refreshments. He took the cup of palm wine offered him and settled a small dish of nuts on his lap, his eyes never leaving the half-naked beauties who served him with pleasant smiles.

He swallowed some wine and met his host's amused look. He cocked his head.

"Ye've made up yer mind, then, never ta return ta England?"

Newton gestured at their immediate surroundings.

"Can you conceive of an occupation there that would pay half as well and afford me as many comforts?"

Gother looked around, and Newton could almost see the wheels turning in the man's head.

"No. But I bin tawd of a proper fortune waitin' on you in London."

Newton doubted that but decided to play along.

"How 'proper'?"

"Four 'underd pown per annum."

Newton whistled. "That would, indeed, be comfortable." He sipped his wine. "But it would take far more than a questionable inheritance to drag me onboard another ship."

Gother seemed to consider that as he took the plum proffered by one of Newton's concubines. He bit into the juicy skin and watched through narrowed eyes as Newton caressed his servant.

"I carry a full crew. You needs do no work, see. You could

lay roun' all day, fishin' an' smoothin' the cat."

"You have a cat?"

Gother grinned. "A yella Tom . . . keeps the rats baity."

Newton smiled. He despised rats—had an almost girlish fear of them.

Both men watched the women retreat to the hut, then Gother continued to press the issue.

"You would lodge in me cabin, dine at me table."

Newton crossed his arms behind his head and lay back, looking up at the swaying palm branches.

"I fear nothing could persuade me from this life, Captain. Not my father, not Manesty, not even a 'proper' inheritance. I am happy here. London no longer beckons me home."

They relaxed in the midday breeze, listening to the women's distant chatter and the buzz of curious dragonflies, until Gother broke the silence.

"Would you wifdraw fer the love of a woman, then?"

He said it casually . . . too casually, Newton thought.

"Fer the love of . . . Miss Mary Catlett?"

Newton sprang out of his hammock and towered over the surprised captain.

"What do you know of Miss Catlett?"

Gother reached inside his flannel jacket and slowly withdrew a small envelope.

"I know she left you this."

Newton reached out shaking fingers and slid the envelope from the captain's hand. The parchment was water stained, his name a blur of black ink. He turned it over. The seal had survived the journey, and he ran his fingers over the monogrammed

*C* stamped into the bloodred wax, the words CATLETT and CHATHAM circling it.

He stood paralyzed with the envelope in his hand, an odd combination of hope and dread coursing through his veins, gripping his heart until it pounded loudly in protest. How many times had he waited patiently on the ship's deck for a return word from her? What life-changing event had compelled her to send a message now—now that he was settled into a distant and separate existence?

He stumbled away from the captain to the far side of an enormous palm. He leaned against the bark, feeling the sweat pour out of him as he worked up the courage to break the seal and read the words that had traveled so far. He finally slipped his thumbnail under the edge of the wax, gently prying it free, then pulled out the folded sheet of laid paper.

He opened it, first seeing the date of *20 June 1746* written in the Italian copperplate style so popular with Englishwomen. He closed his eyes, imagining Mary's skilled hand dipping the quill into the ink, carefully pressing the tip against the cotton page. Then he took a breath, opened his eyes, and read.

> *Dear Mr. Newton,*
> *Two months of Sundays have passed since you left us to return to your warship. It has been a season of many things— doubt, belief, doubt again. War is a good and terrible thing, Jack tells me. But with you mired in it, I struggle to grasp its worth.*
> *Your letters stopped arriving fourteen months ago without explanation. My inquiries into your situation are met with resounding silence. And as I wait for word—are you shipwrecked? are you a prisoner? are you alive?—I find myself on*

*my knees, alternately praying for your safekeeping and quoting Macbeth: "Tomorrow, and tomorrow, and tomorrow, creeps in this petty pace from day to day."*

*I am painfully aware I left you with no intimation, no reason, to hope for any connection with me, save friendship. But if you would come home, if you would make your way to the Chatham parlour of so many happy memories, I believe you would find a new promise there.*

*Yours ever,*
*Miss Mary Catlett*

The words blurred as he read them again and again. *Come home . . . come home . . .* He dragged his arm across his wet eyes, holding back the sobs with great effort. He could not remember the last time he'd shed tears over anyone or anything. He tried to blink them back, but they kept coming.

He folded the paper and slid it back into the envelope. Then he pushed himself away from the palm and marched into his hut. He lifted a large basket off a hook on the wall and carried it into a back room. Boots, pants, shirts, and handkerchiefs went into the pannier, followed by knives, the pistols that would not now duel, and his beloved Euclid—Mary's letter tucked carefully within its pages.

He carried the heavy basket through the front door and over to the captain.

"When do we leave?"

Gother came slowly to his feet, a relieved look on his face.

"Dreckly, I s'pose."

Newton nodded and led the way back through the brushwood to the shoreline, setting a pace that left no breath for speaking.

On the beach McCraig and two crewmen stacked cords of camwood into a flat-bottomed lighter. Without a word Newton joined in, and within a quarter hour the boat was ready to launch for the *Greyhound*.

Newton drew McCraig to the side, shook his hand, and simply said he was leaving with the captain. Then he left the astonished man on the beach and carried his basket onto the loaded boat.

Within an hour the wood was deposited in the ship's hold, the lighter was stored, and all hands prepared to launch, hauling in the anchor and bending the sails.

When the wind caught, Newton moved to the quarterdeck, staring back at McCraig still on the beach, his hands on his hips. The *Greyhound* moved swiftly along the peninsula, tacking south and east until Newton could no longer see the island or the Kittam.

And then he turned his back, leaned against the rail, and dreamt of home.

# CHAPTER

## 12

*Chatham*
*Late March 1747*

Mary stood in the corner of the back parlor with her mouth open, knowing it was unladylike yet unable to force it closed. She looked from face to face—at her mother who glowed with barely contained excitement, at her father who squinted at her in expectation, at Elizabeth who wore the customary loathing for the eldest sibling who *always* got to do *everything*. Young George had actually clapped with the news.

Mary was finding it difficult to put a finger on her mood. She was surprised, yes, but whether pleasantly or dreadfully, she could not say. She closed her mouth and tried to swallow with a tongue that had gone thick and dry. She pried it off the roof of her mouth and spoke.

"London."

They all nodded.

"For the Season."

They nodded again. *Like marionettes,* she thought and felt hysterical laughter bubble up her throat. She sat down hard on the chaise lounge and gripped the creamy cotton covering, crushing the rose pattern in her fists.

Her mother could contain her enthusiasm no longer and spoke in a rush. "They are expecting you within the week, so we must make haste. Six weeks is scant time to assemble a wardrobe of this magnitude, even in London. Oh, Mary! You will be a Churchill for the Season!"

Mary stared at her mother. She was not a Churchill. She was a Catlett. From a Navy port . . . a dockyard town. She unstuck her tongue a second time.

"How . . . how. . . ?"

"Oh!" Her mother burned now with an eagerness to share. "I simply wrote to my cousin, the baroness"—Mary winced at her mother's superior tone when reminding them all of her family's peerage—"and hinted that my eldest daughter could use a change. Her reply was almost immediate. 'Send Mary to us for the Season,' she wrote. 'We would be happy to introduce her.' And that was that!"

Mary looked down at her lap. Her mother had misunderstood her question. *How* could she leave now when the snow had just melted and the tulips had yet to bloom? *How* could she desert the Marine and their herb garden?

Her mother rattled on.

"The roads are atrocious—a sea of mud, so your father will

take you by cutter, and you will arrive in a day. The viscount will follow in a week."

Mary's head snapped up. Alex was a party to this? She mentally shook herself. When had she started calling him "Alex"? She thought hard and supposed somewhere within the past month. Over herbs and conversation in Captain Ward's kitchen, she had come to think of him as anything but a viscount. A viscount did not banter with a revenue man's daughter. A viscount did not discuss his faith and debate biblical truths.

"The viscount."

"Yes, yes." Her mother waved a dismissive hand. "He will be your escort for the Season."

Well. They had it all worked out, didn't they? She stood, ready to refuse them all, when young George spoke up.

"And you'll get to see Jack, won't you?"

Jack. A wave of longing for her brother washed over her. How she missed him and their little adventures. She looked at George's radiant face and tightly sprung body and held out her arms to him. He raced across the room and lunged into her lap, toppling them both onto the chaise. She laughed and snuggled him against her chest.

*I'm going to London, and I'm going to see Jack,* she thought. And that was that.

———

*Berkeley Square, London*

The coach pulled up to *№ 36* Berkeley Square, and Mary peered out with mixed feelings. London—at least what she had seen of it in the half-light of dusk—was either a filthy beast or a grand lady . . . most likely a little of both.

When her father's cutter docked at the wharf fronting the Custom House, the picturesque London Bridge adorned the Thames, and the great dome of St. Paul's Cathedral loomed majestically in the distance. But on the ground the city became a cesspit of sewage, cursing drivers, and coal-blackened sky. Mary wagered she'd held a handkerchief to her nose for nearly an hour until the hackney driver announced they had reached the wide expanse of the Strand. And her arm ached from gripping the leather strap that kept her off the floor of the rocking, jolting coach.

But despite her discomfort, she could not tear her eyes away from the passing views. All along the street, hordes of people in the latest fashions walked, laughed, and shopped. Men in ruffled sleeves and jabots stepped in and out of coffee shops. Women filed one by one out of stores, their hooped skirts as wide as— and, at times, even wider than—the doorways of booksellers and chic shops. The array of fashion was so lavish, Mary began to understand her mother's concerns about assembling a wardrobe. She owned *nothing* fit for London.

The town house now outside her carriage window gave her another pause. Looming up into the darkening sky, *№ 36* was one of an identical row of three-story mansions standing shoulder to shoulder, fronting the wide streets around Berkeley Square. The mellowed bricks glowed against the oil lamps, the reflectors illuminating the ornate front door and elaborate wrought-iron railings.

Mary looked up and down the formal square and wondered,

yet again, what she was doing here.

But at that moment the front door flew open, and a young woman charged onto the sidewalk. Mary knew who she was in an instant—her mother's description was shockingly accurate.

*"Now, your cousin is not beautiful,"* her mother had warned. *"She's short and a bit round and has a wild mane of hair even redder than yours. But she's spirited and immensely popular with both men and women. You will do each other some good."*

Mary opened the carriage door and stepped out just in time to be wrapped in her cousin's pudgy arms.

"Oh, my dear!" exclaimed the little ball of energy squeezing the breath out of her. "You have saved me from a most *dreadfully* tedious Season! What fun we shall have!"

And without another word Miss Churchill pulled her cousin through the gate and the doorway, and Mary only had time to glance over her shoulder at her father before she was dragged into the ground floor entrance hall and up a curving stone staircase. By the light of candles in glass cases, she caught flashes of mahogany doors and woodwork, walls papered in the new "flock" pattern, and a series of portraits in massive frames. Her cousin turned at the top of the stairs, called "Toodle-oo!" to the first-floor maid, and then they were climbing another set of stairs in near darkness, Mary bunching her skirts in her free hand to avoid tripping. At the top and nearly out of breath, Mary followed her cousin down a carpeted hall and into a bedroom where she collapsed into an overstuffed chair and blinked at her surroundings.

Miss Churchill dashed about the airy room, her movements stirring the ethereal blue silk canopy, puffed and tied at each bedpost, and the white sheers trimmed in pale lavender ribbon at each floor-to-ceiling window. Someone had turned down the daffodil-embroidered sheets and fluffed the corn yellow pillows in invitation. Mary took it all in and found herself hoping—sincerely, desperately hoping—this breezy, romantic room, or one exactly like it, would be hers.

Miss Churchill hastened to light an assortment of candles, all in glass cases, until the room was aglow in soft flickering light. Then she stood in front of her cousin, arms folded, eyes narrowed, head tilted in contemplation.

"This will be your room," she began. "And *you* are quite lovely. The auburn hair and blue eyes are a *stunning* combination. Mrs. Frock, my dressmaker—is that not droll? A dressmaker named 'Frock'?—she will simply *squeal* with delight when she sees you! Which will be on the morrow . . . not a moment to lose. We have a social engagement on Saturday, and Easter two weeks hence."

She took a breath and Mary had an overwhelming urge to raise her hand, as if she were back in grammar school.

"You must call me Dorrie, and I will call you Mary—but only in private. In public, I am afraid," and she sighed dramatically, "we will have to be 'Miss.'" She paused suddenly with wide eyes.

"Do you have any questions?"

Mary opened her mouth and, for the first time in a very long time, burst out laughing. She laughed until she was doubled over from the effort and tears streamed down her cheeks. Dorrie joined in, a childlike, almost musical sound bubbling out of her round face.

Mary wiped her eyes and grinned over at her cousin.

"Thank you," she said, and meant it. It was a moment of pure joy, and she felt lighter than she'd felt in a year.

"Now," said Dorrie as she pulled a chair so close their knees touched, "before Mum intrudes, you must tell me everything you can about this viscount."

---

*Saturday, April 4*

Mary stood near the fireplace in the ground-floor fore-parlor, feeling like a fraud.

She ran a hand over her embroidered stomacher. Mrs. Frock had, indeed, squealed at her newest client, clapping her worn hands and mumbling to herself as she laid out bolt after bolt of very fine, very expensive cloth. Mary shuddered to think what her wardrobe was costing the Churchills—"a gift," they had insisted.

The past days had sped by in a whirlwind of measurements and fittings, social instructions and conversations. And through it all, laughing . . . so much laughing. Dorrie was, quite simply, the most naturally entertaining person Mary had ever encountered, including Jack.

Mary was so exhausted from each day's activities, she could hardly recall her father coming into her room early yesterday morning to bid her *adieu*. He'd kissed her forehead and said something about "happiness" and "the captain" and was gone.

It was the subject of Captain Todd that was troubling her now. Try as she might, she could not convince the Churchill ladies there was nothing but friendship between Alex and her. They'd been atwitter for days about "the viscount," as they insisted on calling him, and his arrival, arranging and rearranging the coach seating, debating Mary's best placement in the fore-parlor.

Of course it did not help her case that Alex had planned tonight's outing and had sworn her hosts to secrecy. She'd had no contact with him for a fortnight, had no opportunity to warn him, and now stood dutifully at the fireplace awaiting the moment they would crush the Churchill ladies' romantic dreams.

A knock came at the door. Dorrie raised her chin a notch, sitting even straighter on the edge of the divan, and gave her cousin a comical wink. Then the room went silent as a tomb and the mantel clock ticked ominously; and Mary considered how this whole display was about to be wasted on a Navy captain from Ilfracombe, who'd defaulted into the peerage through a complicated series of births and deaths. He had known his distant cousin, the earl, less than a year. And he assumed the title quite reluctantly.

Alex entered the parlor, and Mary watched with barely contained amusement as her aunt and cousin went all agog at the sight of him. To his credit, he was adorned in a beautiful suit of fine linen, the black of the coat matching his hair and accenting his green eyes. His buff-colored waistcoat, cut in the latest fashion, curved away from his waist, revealing heavily muscled legs in matching breeches. Only the stockings and black leather shoes looked out of place, she thought. He seemed more natural to her in boots.

"Dear heart!" Dorrie exclaimed into the silence, "but you are a terribly handsome man!"

*Well put,* Mary thought, biting her lip to stop the grin from spreading.

The introductions began, Lord Churchill taking pains to use all the correct forms of address with his esteemed guest. Dorrie retreated into polite sophistication at her father's pointed stare, and Lady Churchill was elegance incarnate.

At last Alex was before her, taking her proffered hand with a devilish gleam in his eye. He bent over her hand, murmuring, "Your beauty, Miss Catlett, is like a knife to my . . . breast."

Oh, he was wicked! Bringing up the circumstances of their first meeting when she could not retalia—

She had a thought and smiled prettily. "Why, thank you . . . *Lord Clarendon.*"

There. He had forbidden her to call him by his presumptive title, but she had sworn him to secrecy about the little knife episode. She saw by his narrowed eyes that give and take was, indeed, fair play.

It was only when they were seated in the coach and moving across town that she realized how Alex had sensed her discomfiture as she stood by the fireplace and had sought to distract her with a little repartee. It had worked. She smiled across at him, catching his eye in the candle glow as he regaled the Churchills with descriptions of the earl's house on Grosvenor Square.

In what seemed a short time, the coach came to a halt and Alex handed her down onto a fine, wide thoroughfare, brightly lit and bustling with Londoners in formal dress. Mary took in the imposing brick buildings, the stream of evening traffic and the crowds, and raised an eyebrow at her dashing escort.

"Where are we?"

"The Haymarket."

She looked at him with wide eyes.

"Yes," he laughed. "We are going to the opera."

Her mouth hung open in astonishment. "The opera? It has been my fondest desire to attend the opera!"

"I know." He smiled into her eyes. "You told me."

She shook her head, speechless. He tucked her hand into his arm and waltzed her through the center brick archway of the King's Theatre.

Inside, Alex presented each of their party with a subscription token, white in color and etched in black with "King's Theatre Haymarket 1746–47." Mary turned the token over and over in her gloved hand as she tried to take in the spectacle of London's elite milling about the gilded lobby, nodding across the room, whispering behind elaborate fans. Whatever the opera, she thought the real performance was unfolding right before her in the entrance hall. And she was aware of an excessive amount of attention directed her way. She heard Alex sigh and knew he detected it, too. With a brisk "Shall we?" he escorted their party up the grand staircase and into Box No. 6—the earl's box.

Mary settled onto the red velvet chair, expertly whisking aside the silk waterfall train of her blue-green gown as she blinked across at the enormous hooped chandelier suspended from an ornately painted ceiling of plump clouds and cherubs. A hidden orchestra played an overture, the music in tempo with the thump of the pulse in her neck.

This was where Handel presented his oratorios—*Esther,*

*Samson,* the *Messiah.* This was where Scarlatti staged his operas and Terradellas introduced his wind instruments. She'd read the reviews over and over again in Fog's *Weekly Journal,* always dreaming but never believing she would be here.

Someone handed her a program, and she dragged her gaze away from the pageantry to read, *"Bellerofonte,* by Francesco Vanneschi and Domingo Terradellas." Her breath caught. Terradellas was still in residence. And then the next surprise—"Italian Tenor Borosini sings 'Giobate'." Borosini! Back in London!

The overture concluded with a flourish, then *ting, ting, ting!* rang the prompter's bell. Eight o'clock. The crowd settled and the massive crimson curtains rose steadily, and every part of Mary's being glittered with the theatre's brilliance. And she had a very frank, very distinct feeling that nothing in her life would ever again match this moment of pure delight . . . of pure emotion.

Each of the three acts ran its course, the classic Greek tale of love and jealousy and an impossible quest unfolding on the elaborate stage. Enthusiastic applause greeted Borosini's every entrance as the King of Lycia, the tenor flexing his extraordinary voice, traversing and leaping up and down his two-octave range. And at the end, when Bellerofonte fell from his flying horse to his death and Pegasus transformed into a constellation, the heavy curtains dropped in a *whoosh* of scarlet and gold, and the crowd erupted in cheers and ovations.

And Mary sat like a stone in the earl's box, overwhelmed by the experience, thinking to herself that it was all too much . . . too much.

She could hear Dorrie and her parents raving to the patrons

in Box 5, invitations to late suppers, calls for the viscount's attention. She knew the musical interlude was about to begin, saw out of the corner of her eye fashionable society preening and flirting whilst they milled about the luxurious room. And she just wanted them all to go away—to leave her in this moment. Alone.

But it was an impossibility. When she finally looked away from the crimson curtain, she turned her head and gazed directly into Alex's gentle green eyes. She wanted to tell him what this night, this experience, had meant to her. She wanted to explain the feelings that had coursed through her over the past hours, how the music had called to her and how her heart had answered. She had an urge to throw her arms around him—like she would with Jack—and unashamedly rest in the embrace of one who understood the longings of her heart. But she felt that if she did anything, even spoke at this moment, she would be undone.

So she looked at her friend, her own eyes glittering with tears, and mouthed the only words, wholly inadequate, that she could say. "Thank you."

———————

*Easter Sunday, April 19*

Mary rolled to the edge of the bed and noticed two things straightaway: she'd left a candle burning and the mattress was dipping alarmingly on one side. She maneuvered onto an elbow and came instantly awake.

"Jack!"

Her brother perched on the side of her bed, grinning. He put a finger to his lips and leaned in close, whispering.

"I've brought you some clothes. Dress quickly. Adventure is afoot."

She sprang out of bed and donned the boy's clothing as Jack handed each piece to her—breeches, shirt, waistcoat, greatcoat. She noted even in her haste that each item was too large for her. She glanced at her brother in the low light. The boy was becoming a man.

He handed over her riding boots and a Monmouth that had seen better days. She moved toward the bedroom door, tucking her braided hair up under the hat, but Jack caught her by the arm and pulled her over to the window. She squinted at him in the darkness.

"We're two floors up."

He threw a leg over the sill and was soon standing in midair. She peered out the window and then at him.

"You *stole* a ladder?"

"It was already here. I noticed it late last night when I arrived and simply *moved* it."

Mary shook her head and climbed out after him, descending into a garden fragrant with turned earth and new blossoms. In a thrice Jack laid the ladder on the ground and was pulling her through the back streets and around the mansion mews until they crossed Piccadilly and hunkered down at the edge of Green Park.

Mary leaned against the iron fence, catching her breath, admiring the stillness of a usually bustling thoroughfare. She turned to her brother.

"So what fascination brings us out here in the dead of night?"

"A duel takes place at dawn just there on the Queen's Walk." And he jutted with his chin toward the fashionable venue.

"A duel? On Easter Sunday? That's . . . that's . . . scandalous!"

"Yes," he grinned. "Delightfully so."

Jack stood and moved along the fence, contemplating the massive trees that lined the Queen's Walk. He returned several times to a single tree, then beckoned for her.

He cupped his hands, and she gripped his shoulders but hesitated before giving him her booted foot.

"Pistols or swords?"

"Swords. They don't want to kill each other, just demand a little satisfaction."

She sighed. "However do you learn about these things?"

"It never fails to astonish me what people will disclose in the darkness of a carriage."

She stepped into his hands, bent her knee, and was propelled onto the low heavy bough of a sprawling oak. Jack was soon beside her, and she followed him up and out onto a limb with a spectacular view of the walkway. They sat close together, talking of school and home, watching the sky lighten until Jack threw up a hand for silence.

Four men approached from the north and walked right under the oak tree. Mary recognized no one from the grim group, but two of them wore the trappings of the upper class, and one carried a physician's bag. They stopped forty yards away, two abreast in the middle of the paved walk. Minutes later a similar group approached from the south. Mary squinted through the first light, drawn by the familiar gait of a tall man in leather breeches and riding boots.

*No* . . . she thought, her heart racing. She squinted harder, desperate to be wrong. But in a moment she let out a groan, and Jack gripped her shoulder hard enough to leave a bruise. She turned to him with wide eyes, and he mouthed, "What?"

She stared at her brother, jaw slack, then back at the group. He shook her, and she looked back at him.

"I . . . I know . . . one of those men."

Now Jack squinted into the morning, his gaze flicking over each man. He turned to her.

"Which one?"

She swallowed hard and tapped his breeches, mouthing, "Leather."

They watched as that man stepped forward, drawing a dueling sword from a scabbard clipped to his waist. A man from the first group did likewise, and Mary jerked, nearly losing her balance.

Jack grabbed her around the waist and pinned her to the spot with a heavy leg and the sternest look she'd ever seen on his handsome face. He put his mouth so close to her ear that she felt, rather than heard, his words.

"We *cannot* be discovered. Do you understand?"

She nodded, but everything in her wanted to leap from the tree and halt this madness. She watched the men meet in the middle, exchange swords, and make a careful inspection of the other's handle and blade.

Jack whispered in her ear. "Who is he?"

She put her mouth to his ear. "He is . . . Captain Todd of the Royal Navy."

Jack's eyes grew wide at that and he mouthed, "The viscount?"

She fought the urge to explain how Alex despised that title and simply nodded.

Jack put his lips to her ear once more. "Not to worry. He is only acting as the dueler's second."

Mary relaxed a little and studied Alex a bit closer. It was difficult to see his face in the half-light, but his jawline and stance were rigid with fury. She had never seen him angry, and watching him now shed a new light on his status in the Navy. He was not a man to be trifled with.

The seconds traded swords again, and Alex spoke in a clear voice.

"To first blood, then?"

The nobleman in the first party laughed and spat out, "No."

Alex's eyes never left those of the other second who shook his head . . . a bit sadly, Mary thought. Alex cocked his head to the side and spoke in the same calm, clear manner.

"We will not fight to the death. There is no honor in that."

Alex stared down the second until the nobleman gave a lusty sigh and threw up his hands.

"Very well. The devil hang the both of you. I'll just *cripple* the bloke." And he threw off his coat and marched forward, snatching the sword from his second's hand.

Alex retreated to his party, handing over the sword and speaking intently. His nobleman nodded once, removed his coat, and took a stance. Alex moved to the center, held a white handkerchief aloft and, after a nod from the other second, dropped it.

The swordplay was fantastic. Mary thought the two noble-men well-matched, each attacking and defending in double time—parry, reposte . . . parry, reposte. The ring of steel on steel was almost musical, the tempo steady as a metronome.

Mary leaned toward Jack, her eyes never leaving the combatants.

"For what do they fight?"

"A woman . . . of course." She could hear the grimace in his voice.

The noblemen battled on, nicking each other here and there, spots of blood showing through tiny rips in their clothing. They moved in straight lines across an imaginary circle, thrusting with remarkable speed, their breath puffing into the brisk spring air.

Then Alex's nobleman executed a rather balletic move, lunged and pierced his opponent high on the sword arm. The injured man staggered back, reaching for his falling sword with his left hand. But his opponent was too quick, and he found his left arm run through as well. The sword clattered to the walk-way, and the injured man looked from it to his opponent in astonishment.

Blood seeped into his white shirt, spreading down his sleeves. And still neither man moved nor spoke. Alex approached from the side, catching his nobleman's eye, shaking his head no. Mary held her breath, hoping this would be the end of it.

The injured man dropped to his knees, his head down, but in a surprise move he grabbed his sword and lunged. Toward Alex.

Mary's scream was drowned out in the shouting from all

parties as Alex spun away and held a dagger to the man's throat. The injured man dropped the sword, and his opponent stood on the blade, the tip of his own sword resting against the man's heart.

Alex stepped back and his nobleman spoke loud enough for all to hear.

"You broke the code, sir—attacking my second in such a manner." He placed the sword tip under his opponent's chin, forcing the man to look up.

"You dishonor the nobility. Remove yourself from this town . . . and stay away from my sister." He kicked the injured man's sword toward his visibly worried second and walked away.

The groups disbursed soon afterward, Jack and Mary watching the injured man refuse medical treatment and try to walk on his own, stumbling and falling before accepting assistance right under their tree. They sat on their branch, silent, watching the sky lighten and waiting for an all clear.

Mary had just turned to her brother and drawn a breath to speak when a familiar voice floated up to them from the street.

"Come down."

Mary looked downward, mortified. Alex leaned against the fence, his arms crossed and a commanding look on his face. She spun around to Jack, who shrugged and started his descent. She lingered on the branch, feeling trapped and oddly liberated at the same time.

Jack hit the ground like a cat and padded over to Alex.

"Hullo," he said cheerily, hand outstretched. "Jack Catlett."

Alex reacted just as Jack had doubtless planned, Mary

thought. He stood away from the fence and shook the boy's hand, eyebrows raised.

"Catlett."

Jack nodded. "Of the Chatham Catletts." He smiled and looked up into the tree. "I believe you know my sister."

Alex look up with such a painful mixture of expressions that Mary felt sorry for him instead of herself. Alexander Todd was rarely speechless, but this particular conclusion to the morning's events seemed to be too much. He stared at her in silence for so long that she moved to descend the tree just to help him recover.

She hung from the lower branch and was surprised to feel hands around her waist, lowering her to the ground. She looked up and into Alex's bemused face. He held her in place, and she looked him over.

"You are all right, then?"

He nodded as he took in the battered hat and outsized coat, the breeches and boots. And still he did not speak.

She drew a quick breath and resorted to etiquette. "I believe you've met my brother."

Alex looked at the ground and began to laugh. It was one of those deep chortles that started in the belly and burst out through a wide smiling mouth.

Mary shot a significant look at Jack, who marched over, grabbed her by the hand, and pulled her away from the slightly hysterical viscount.

"Well, then," Jack said as they inched along the fence. "We'll see you at Easter dinner, shall we?" And they were off without an answer . . . just another gust of booming glee.

# CHAPTER

## ◄ 13 ►

*London*
*Early May 1747*

I t was just like living in the pages of a novel.

Mary smiled across at the dashing lead character playing the dual roles tonight of Captain Alexander Todd of the Royal Navy and Viscount Clarendon, the Heir Presumptive of the fourth earl of Clarendon. He was deep in thought, squinting up and out of the carriage, trying to counter her last quotation with one that would finally stump her.

The game—and the fantasy—had begun when he'd arrived at the Churchill's manse, dressed in Navy finery but traveling in none other than the earl's plush landau. She'd stood on the doorstep, staring at the vehicle, the Clarendon coat of arms emblazoned on the glazed door, the matched pair of ebony steeds, the liveried driver, the black hood split and folded back to reveal the opulent inhabitants of the opulent carriage.

Then she'd looked at Alex—wigged for once, resplendent in his officers' trappings of blue and white and gold, the buckles on his shoes sparkling in the late-afternoon sunlight. And then she'd glanced down at her own attire—the deep blue skirt of her linen mantua, hooped in the latest style, fanning out from the open waist to reveal the creamy petticoat embroidered with horizontal rows of blue irises. *"An Admiralty dinner party,"* he'd told her. *"Nothing elaborate."* Her shoulders sagged under the mantelet. Her gown was lovely, but certainly not opulent enough for the earl's landau.

She'd raised a troubled brow at her escort, and he'd responded with a lift of his own brow, a lazy smile creeping up to his eyes.

"In London, all worlds collide."

Indeed.

He'd handed her into the carriage, and she'd settled onto the velvet seat facing backward, preferring the view of where she'd just been rather than where she was headed.

They'd clip-clopped along in companionable silence, Mary telling herself not to worry about her attire, cheering herself with memories of the Churchill ladies' praise, until Alex drew her attention by quoting Syrus.

"'An agreeable companion on a journey is as good as a carriage.'"

She'd smirked and looked about, noting with not a little irritation the stir caused by the landau and its occupants, and countered with a Russian proverb: "'Gossip needs no carriage.'"

Now, as Alex worked on a riposte, Mary considered their

destination. At the north end of Whitehall, adjacent to the Houses of Parliament, was the Admiralty—the unpretentious brick and stone center of British sea power. Lord John Russell, the fourth duke of Bedford and the reigning First Lord of the Admiralty, was holding a dinner party. He was popular and successful but preferred the company of contemporaries who did not take their status so seriously. He was enthralled by the reluctant Viscount Clarendon and had endeared himself to the man by steadfastly referring to him as Captain Todd.

This was the extent of the information Alex had deemed essential for her preparation. He did not wish for her to fixate on titles and precedence, as Lord John Russell did not. It would be a small party—no more than ten in attendance. She should listen carefully to each introduction, then mimic it.

Mary fingered the trim on her reticule—the same fabric that matched the ruching on her bodice that matched the color of the embroidered irises that complemented her blue eyes. She smiled. The fashions, the entertainments, the intrigues—simply *preparing* for the London Season was surreal to her. Each day here she felt less like Mary Catlett and more like a character in a book. A good book, though . . . a good read.

Her lead character caught her eye then, observing her happiness and returning it with crinkling eyes and relaxed pleasure. His steady gaze said to her, *Celebrate your delight . . . be whole.* It was a long and agreeable moment interrupted by the gradual halt of the landau and the driver bounding down to place the steps and open the low door.

Alex stepped out first, turning to help Mary to the ground. She gripped his warm hand with her gloved one, smiling contentedly for just five steps before the fantasy was crushed by reality.

Ahead of her, queued along the high brick wall to the Admiralty's single entrance, was a line of mutilated creatures. Disfigured by war, in various stages of military dress, the men limped and hopped forward—some on wooden legs, others on crutches. Some missing an arm, some a hand, some with an eye out and a sleeve empty to the shoulder.

It was the gruesome consequence of war that did not make an appearance in Berkeley Square.

She felt Alex pulling her away from the macabre sight, coaxing her toward the entrance. But he did not understand the depth of her horror—the realization that another dear sailor might return from the war in any one of these conditions. She met the eye of every crippled man who would meet hers. She took a long look at what might be her next glimpse of John Newton.

And then they were through the cobbled courtyard, under the portico, and just inside the buff-colored entrance hall. They faced each other, faces flushed for very different reasons. Alex gripped her hands.

"I am . . ." He shook his head. "I will speak to the Admiral—"

She interrupted him with a vicious shake of her own head.

"Those men have suffered enough. It would do the citizenry well to see the effects of their war." She smoothed her features and squeezed his hand. "It was a momentary shock. Nothing more."

But that was a lie. Mary glided up the principal staircase, her hand tucked into the arm of her handsome escort, chin up. Beneath the serene façade broiled a myriad of emotions—the panicked struggle to remember John's face, just as it was that last Christmas . . . an overwhelming desire to pore over his letters, filling her heart with his bold declarations . . . and a renewed determination to find the sailor who haunted her dreams. London was the busiest seaport in the world. Someone in this city had the answers to her questions.

They paused in front of the great oaken doors to the board room. Alex handed the steward his embossed invitation, upon which the man confirmed their names, flung open the doors, rapped his ebony staff twice, and cried, "Captain Alexander Todd and Miss Catlett!"

They stepped into a great chamber of dark oak paneling and lofty white ceiling. The long and elaborately dressed dinner table seemed dwarfed in the center, yards away from the great fireplace and trio of massive windows that flanked it. Straight ahead, on the north wall, was an enormous globe mounted between two tall cases of leather-bound books.

Mary had the distinct feeling she was a guest of the board room rather than a guest of the Lord High Admiral. The members of the board would come and go, but the noble room in which so much of England's history was made seemed to whisper, "I will remain."

Within moments the introductions began. Lady John Russell, a young and sprightly woman, spirited them around the chamber, presenting "Sirs" and "Ladies" and "Lords." But it was Captain Manesty, a portly yet elegant man, who drew Mary's attention.

His brows shot up at her name, and he hardly waited for the complete introduction before asking, "Of the Chatham Catletts?"

At her nod he pressed further. "Daughter of George and Elizabeth Catlett?"

She inclined her head again, and Manesty turned to Alex.

"Might I steal away your guest, Captain Todd?"

As they appeared to know each other, Alex did not hesitate and handed her over with the barest wink.

Manesty drew her toward the globe, explaining how the pointer of the massive wind-dial mounted above it was connected to a vane on the roof. "Northeast," he proclaimed, then tilted his head and studied her.

"Last summer," he began, "I had a brief encounter with a Marine—a physician who had made your acquaintance in Chatham."

"Captain Ward," Mary offered with a smile.

"The very one."

Manesty seemed to struggle with what he wanted to say next. When he finally looked at her, it was with the kindest of expressions—much like a loving parent.

"Captain Ward gave me a letter—a letter written by you, he said, and addressed to a young sailor."

"John Newton." His name passed her lips in a whisper, and her eyes felt hot and wet.

Manesty nodded. "I sent that letter almost immediately with one of my southbound ships."

She waited, barely breathing, feeling every stay in her corset.

"Ten months have passed with no word." Manesty leaned in.

"But I will not give him up for lost! Will you?"

She shook her head, but a tear escaped down her cheek.

Manesty adjusted their position so that she faced the wind-dial and he faced the room. She forced herself to breathe deeply, compose her features, be a lady.

"Two days hence," he said in a soothing voice, "I make my way to Wapping, the site of John's childhood. An old woman resides there who is rumored to have news of every Wapping sailor on a vessel—better news than even Lloyd's."

He took her hand. "Will you accompany me there?"

She nodded and he smiled.

"Good. I will call upon your hosts tomorrow and settle it."

Dinner was announced and Alex was at Mary's side, escorting her to the elegant table. She sat to the right of Lady John Russell, facing the windows full of early evening sun, listening to the forceful *tick-tock* of the fine grandfather clock.

And the room of so many tidings, of victories and mutinies, of accusations and acquittals, seemed to tuck itself around her, enfolding her troubled heart and mind, whispering, *Endure . . . remain . . .*

———

The domed candles on the earl's landau cast a soft inviting light as Mary swayed with the carriage's rhythm, lost in thought. She feared she had not been good company at the admiral's dinner. She had murmured the correct responses, smiled at the appropriate moments . . . but her mind had been elsewhere. Her mind had been in Wapping.

In two days she might be closer to an answer—an answer she

might not want. And what would she do with the information? Would she simply accept it, good or bad? Would she carry it around, seared on her heart as she danced and chatted her way through the events of the Season? Would she let it color her days, her weeks, her future?

"Mary."

She slowly focused on the handsome face across from her. Alex. Alex was in the present and might very well be part of her future, if . . .

"You can tell me about him."

She stared at her friend, her gallant escort, wanting to weep for the gentleness in his voice. He leaned forward.

"I know only enough to help Ward and Manesty gather information. But I can tell you from experience—it is a heavy burden to carry alone."

*Oh, the awful truth in that,* she thought. She considered the open expression on his face and took a breath.

"His mother . . . was stricken with consumption and died in my home. Our mothers were cousins and good friends. I was just a child." She licked her lips.

"He came to visit years later." She looked down at her clasped hands.

"I don't really . . . know him." *Not like I know you,* she wanted to explain. And didn't.

But everything she had said sounded to her own ears like an apology, as if she was trying to beg pardon for caring so much about the writer of a few letters . . . letters she could show no one, and especially not to Alex. She mentally shook herself.

She needed to focus on the issue at hand. A man was missing. Somewhere, someone knew his whereabouts. She would use every resource at her disposal, every means to find him.

And so she told her friend, the Navy captain, the viscount, every detail she could remember about John Newton. The candlelight danced across the landau's luxurious trappings as she poured out her heart to the man she sensed hoped to hold it one day. It was a candid risk—it could cost her everything and gain her nothing.

She only hoped she wasn't chasing a ghost.

# CHAPTER

## ⊰ 14 ⊱

*Wapping, South London*

F or the first time in a very long time, Joseph Manesty felt
powerless.

He sat across from the young beauty, studying her profile as
she stared out at nothing, seeing but not seeing the fascinating
sights along the Thames. The waterman rowed them in and out
of traffic, his language as colorful as the red boat he sculled
through the murky water, but Miss Catlett reacted to none of it.

Manesty understood love and he understood loss. But he'd
experienced them as absolutes, not as lingering questions tapping, relentlessly tapping, on the heart. He wanted to reassure
this woman that Anthony Gother was one of his finest captains,
as determined on his mission to find John Newton as he was to
make a profitable trade. He wanted to regale her with tales of
Gother's cunning, of his penchant to lighten tense moments

with an Irish saying . . . in a Bristol accent, no less. He wanted to say these things, but he did not. He knew she'd listen politely but hear nothing.

Silence from the Atlantic roared ever louder.

And there was the sticky matter of Captain Todd. Manesty was in no way a matchmaker, but if he ever thought two people perfectly suited for each other, it was the captain and Miss Catlett. Beyond the striking couple they made—she with her porcelain skin and auburn tresses, he with his dark and handsome countenance—was a meeting of like minds and spirits.

The captain was the very image of his father, a man Manesty knew from his own seafaring days, a quiet and steady sailor from North Devon, lost in his prime at sea. The son had inherited his father's visage and aptitude, his humility and passion for literature. And the son, like the father, loved the Lord in his own gentle way.

John Newton, however, was an enigma. Motherless at six, fatherless most of his life, he was like a ship without a rudder. Clearly, John was intelligent, but he lacked ambition, bristled at discipline, and—like his father—eschewed religion. Still, Manesty loved the boy—thought of him as his own son. But he could not recommend him . . . not to a lady like Miss Catlett.

Therein lay his involvement. Manesty knew, as did Captain Todd, that the lovely young woman who had captured both their hearts would not easily relinquish the childhood dream of John Newton. They could help her with the facts, but the choice would be hers. So he made his way to Wapping to find answers in the rough and impoverished borough of John's beginning.

The waterman announced their destination and banked at the foot of the Old Wapping Stairs. Manesty stepped out and helped his charge onto the uneven stones. He felt a sudden urge to pray, but for what, he could not say. He looked toward the street and settled on a petition for the old woman. *Let her speak peace, Lord,* he prayed. *Grace and peace.*

––––––––––

Mary stood on Wapping Street, doing her best not to gawk at the little man, at the left side of his mouth permanently drawn up to meet the skin over what used to be his eye, across from a nose like a burlap potato. Though he was forced to speak through the ragged opening, his words were fluid and clear.

"Yeh'll be wantin' the Widow Bailey, then." And he nodded toward a line of brick row houses lurking tall, thin, and unimaginative across the street. "Go ter the red door. Yeh'll be findin' 'er at the top o' the stairs, lookin' out tha' window."

Mary spied the red door and looked skyward. Four stories up, in what must surely be the attic, was a small, perfectly round window set into a bright white molding and framed with red bricks . . . a sunburst atop a drab existence.

"She leaves tha' window twice a week fer church or ta walk the docks an' take in mendin' from the lightermen an' wharfingers. 'At's how she gets the news."

Mary smiled and nodded her thanks, moving to stand directly across from the red door. Manesty thanked the man and offered a shilling for his help. He pocketed it swiftly and called out after them.

"Now, don' be callin' 'er *widow* or she'll be tellin' ya nuthin'.

'Er husband an' son set sail more 'n thirty years past an' never come back. But she thinks they will." He shook his head and shuffled on, muttering, "She thinks they will."

Mary let the man's words ring in her ears as she stood gazing across the filthy street at the old brick house. It had the look of every house along the waterfront—the first floor graced only by a solid-looking door with a red tide line painted across the bricks a foot above it, two small windows on the second and third floors, and the round window at the top. The bricks were chipped and faded, weathered as only sweeping gales coming up the river could batter clay and mortar. The windows, coated with a thick layer of salt, seemed to have given up the fight to shine and reflect the spring sun.

The worn look of the place made the red door and round window more shocking in their intensity, for both bore the look of fresh paint, the polished brass of the door handle glowing warm and inviting. Someone took pains to create a beacon along the mighty river.

They crossed the street and Manesty knocked firmly on the paneled door. After a moment a face peered out at them through the single cut-glass pane, and a Cockney voice called out, "'Oo moit ya be, and what be yer business?"

"Captain Joseph Manesty and Miss Catlett," Manesty answered. "We've come to speak to Mrs. Bailey about a young sailor."

The ensuing silence stretched so long that Manesty raised his hand to knock again. But the door opened just then to reveal a young woman. She could not have passed her sixteenth year, yet her face was already seamed with the daily cares of poor living—

trouble and want always at the forefront of her dockside existence.

She beckoned them into a room lit only by the light from the open door. She looked past them into the street, nodded in satisfaction, then closed the door and threw the bolt, plunging them into a dimness unusual for midday.

She tucked a wayward strand of lank brown hair behind an ear and addressed Mary.

"Very top o' the stairs, then up the ladder, ma'am." And she gave an awkward little curtsy.

Mary smiled and stepped immediately to a stair lit from a thick window on the first-floor landing. Manesty moved to follow, but the young woman blocked his way.

"No fellows allowed above, Cap'n."

Mary paused with her foot on the first step and looked at Manesty, surprised and a little leery of continuing alone. Manesty frowned in disapproval, but the woman would not budge from the path to the stairs.

"Not without 'er 'usband 'ome. 'Twouldn't be proper now, would it?"

Mary considered their predicament for only a moment. She had not come this close in her quest for information to be waylaid by etiquette.

"Very well," she said and shot Manesty a look she hoped conveyed her determination to proceed, with or without him. After a moment he nodded.

Mary turned and started up the steep stair, lifting her skirt and planting each foot carefully on the cracked and uneven steps. At the first landing she made the turn and heard the young woman's next demand.

"'Ave a seat, Cap'n.'"

She continued up, focusing on each step in the dim light. When she reached the next landing, she glanced around for the ladder. What she noticed, instead, was that no decorations or artwork graced the drab walls of the little house. The walls were not painted cheerful colors, if they held any paint at all on the gray surface. This was not a place for living, she concluded with a sad heart . . . it was a place for surviving.

She spied the ladder in a dark corner and the small opening above it. She removed her hat, tucked her skirt into her waistband, and started the climb. *Thank goodness for Jack and all his childish dares,* she thought as she gripped each rung in an experienced hand and ascended into the attic.

When her shoulders cleared the opening, a hand reached out to her. Mary gripped it and stepped into the room with surprising ease. She released her skirt and looked up.

She was in a cozy space, simply furnished with a faded rag rug beside a sturdy cot, a small table graced with a lamp, bowl, and spoon, a three-legged stool, and a single high-backed chair placed next to the round window. The window was most unusual, remarkably smooth in the center and beveled at the edges, letting in the light in both direct and refractory patterns, giving the room a cathedral-like glow.

A delicate woman of indeterminate age took her seat before the window, retrieved a worn shirt from a basket on the stool, and began to mend. Her short gown was plum-colored and impeccable, the striped linen apron tied so perfectly the ends met in her lap. As the widow did not speak, Mary took a moment to smooth her skirts and really observe her.

She had the creamy complexion and fine features of the nobility, the ash blond hair just visible under her linen cap thick and twisted up into a bun. She sat with an erectness that would have pleased any governess, and her long fingers moved the needle through the fabric with practiced ease. If not for the skin of her worn hands, she might have passed for a woman twenty years younger.

Mary moved toward the woman and broke the first rule of decorum: speaking to an elder without first being spoken to. "I've come to inquire about John Newton."

The old woman looked up sharply, flashing intelligent blue eyes, and only her Irish accent gave away her labor status.

"The merchant skipper from Red Lyon Street? He'd be with the Royal Africa Company now. He made summat o' his life, didn't he?" She glanced out the window. "Yeah, he did. 'Cept with tha' boy . . ." Her voiced trailed off and her hands stilled as she stared into the sky.

Mary leaned forward. "You speak of the eldest son of the same name?" The widow seemed to ignore her in her reverie, but Mary pressed for a response. "You know of him?"

The silence stretched between them, and Mary thought she may have trampled on all decorum when, without turning, the widow spoke in a dreamy voice.

"He was . . . diff'rent, tha' boy—sharp, he was. Took ta learnin' like mos' boys take ter the sea." The old woman shook her head. "The sea 'twas his undoin'."

Mary held her breath, then whispered, "He is . . . then, his ship has . . ." But she could not say the words. And the widow would not say them for her.

"The sea took his ma—to Chatham . . . ter die from the sickness. Then the sea took his pa—away from here and t' another wife. I watched the boy some . . . we all did, didn't we, from time to time. I watched him git taller and smarter. An' then I stood on the ol' stairs and watched him sail down the river with his pa 'til they was los' in the mist."

The widow returned her attention to the linen shirt in her lap.

Mary took a breath and asked the question. "And what became of the son, madam?"

"The sea took him, lass . . . just as it took me men." She smiled in reflection. "They wen' away at Easter time, when the tides were high. Husbands an' sons . . . the sea calls ta them like a siren's song."

"But is he . . . dead? Is John Newton dead?" Mary's voice came out on a whimper, and she pressed her fingertips to her lips to still the outburst she felt so near the surface.

The widow paused, then placed her mending in the basket, cleared the stool, and held out a hand. Mary rushed forward, grasped the hand, and collapsed on the stool at the widow's feet. She looked down, biting her lip, fighting for control.

The old woman placed a hand under Mary's chin and tilted her face up. "Is he dead, yeh want ta know. Well, only the Lor' knows that, lass, don' he? I will tell yeh this—John Newton's ship still sails 'til we hear diffren'."

Mary searched the wise and peaceful face of this remarkable woman and asked the deeper question in her heart. "How do you live with the not knowing?"

The woman sat back and pondered that question for a long moment, studying Mary's face, meeting her eyes.

"Outside this window, there is doubt. 'Yer son is dead,' they say. But they don' really know now, do they? They git the same information as me an' think the wors'." She frowned and shook her head.

"But what does the Proverb say? 'Hope deferred maketh the heart sick: but when the desire cometh, it is a tree of life.' On this side o' the window, I see me husband and son livin' in a land far from here, shipwrecked maybe, livin' as best they can 'til another boat comes ta bring 'em home."

The widow stared deep into Mary's eyes.

"So if yeh believe, lass—really believe—yeh'll see John Newton agin, yeh'll have ta find yerself a window. And then, yeh watch an' trust the Lor' will bring him home . . . will bring yer tree of life.

"I canna live without tha' hope." She turned her head toward the sunlight. "I canna live without the window."

Mary studied the woman's profile, so elegant and patrician it seemed carved of marble. The eyes stared unblinking through the beveled glass, and Mary realized the interview was over.

She stood and took in the widow's view. It was breathtaking. For as far as she could see, ships of every size traversed the great highway of the river. Sails swelled, flags flapped, masts and colors ever changing with the tide. She could hear the men shouting on the decks but could not make out the words.

The river was full of life. The river was full of hope.

Mary climbed back down the ladder, then the stairs, and had

her hand on the knob of the red door before she remembered Manesty. He stood in the dim room, his hat in his hands, a question on his face. She shook her head, and they left together without a word.

The tide had gone out, and they climbed down the slippery stones of the Old Wapping Stairs, the walls rising dark and moss-covered around them. Mary stood on the rough bank watching Manesty call for a waterman, overwhelmed by the smell of shipping and the noise of sailors. She watched a group of grubby boys playing on the rude stone causeway left bare from the outgoing tide. She tried to imagine John in this world, on this muddy shore.

The waterman banked and she climbed into the colorful boat, sitting to face downriver. As the little vessel dodged a mass of larger ships, she kept her eye on the shoreline, on the peak of a row house and its little round window.

She tried to imagine herself sitting at her own attic window years from now, waiting . . . longing. Could she do it? Could she persevere inside that attic room, year after year, watching the seasons change, watching the children grow as her heart crumbled bit by bit? Did she really want that kind of existence?

*No,* she decided and sat up straighter.

All of them—she, Manesty, the Marine—had done everything they could to find John Newton. It was up to the Lord now to bring the man home or bring a peace to her heart.

So. The Season began on the morrow, and she would rejoice in it. She would be swept up with the masses in Covent Garden and Piccadilly, drive sedately through Hyde Park, engage in stimulating conversations over chocolate. And she would do it all on the arm of Captain Alexander Todd.

She turned her head and smiled at Manesty, and he returned it with visible relief. It was not what she had come for, but she had her answer. There was more to life than waiting on a ghost.

# CHAPTER

## 15

Gabon River Estuary, Western Africa
Summer 1747

Newton blinked up at the ship's main mast in a rum-filled haze. The boom extending from it looked like an eerie crucifix in the pale moonlight, and into his head popped unbidden the verse:

> Alas, and did my Savior bleed?
> And did my Sov'reign die?
> Would he devote that sacred head
> For such a one as I?

He surged to his feet, cursing Isaac Watts and those wretched hymns that were lodged in his brain from childhood. And then he cursed old Barley and his penchant for singing the Twenty-third Psalm when he was half seas over. Which they all were just now.

He snatched the hefty seashell of rum from Barley, interrupting the Psalm, and proposed a toast.

"Sweethearts and wives," he slurred as he dribbled the amber liquor down his throat.

The crew glared back at him. For their own reasons they so despised the Navy they spurned even the officers' traditional toast. He tossed the shell into the air. *Well, the devil take them,* he thought. It was Saturday night and a fine toast, regardless of its origins.

One of the Portuguese crew Newton liked to call Jack "Celso"—"tall" in Latin—caught the shell, filled it with gin, and spewed out his toast.

"Quando o vinho desce, as palavras sobem."

Newton grinned. He knew enough Portuguese to translate that one. *When wine goes down, words climb up.*

And so the drinking game continued. Pass the shell, propose a toast, down the grog. Last man standing wins.

Newton leaned his spinning head against a ladder. A little more than three months on the *Greyhound* and he was resorting to puerile games to break the monotony. The ship had sailed half a day south of Turner's Peninsula before he'd discovered only three of the crew were English—and those three were more likely to quote Irish proverbs and superstition than Latin and Virgil.

He tapped his forehead against the salt-caked wood. Unrelenting discontent . . . he was cursed with it. What would a journey to London solve?

Old Pete had the shell. "The wind that blows, the ship that goes, and the lass that loved a sailor."

Newton closed his eyes. Mary—the lass that loved . . . Well. That emotion was yet to be declared. To *this* sailor, at any rate. He pushed away from the ladder, banishing the thought of his one passion, his one dream crushed by another, and stumbled into center deck.

"Gentlemen," he bowed with a flourish. "Le pas de deux."

And he began to dance about the half deck like a madman, skylarking around them and through them, goaded by their catcalls and clumsy clapping to an uneven rhythm. He danced as everything they said he was—the degenerate, the rake, the riotous buccaneer. He spun to the rail and threw his arms wide, thinking he might cartwheel his way back across, when the wind caught his hat and blew it overboard.

He howled in indignation until he spied the fickle item resting peacefully in the moonlight in the boat moored below. He was half over the rail, intending to drop into the tender, when strong hands hauled him back on deck.

"Are you daft?" Old Pete had him by the collar. "You can't swim, man!"

"Swim!" Newton pointed, the tip of his finger weaving about. "I'll just step over and snatch the hat and—"

"That boat's twenty feet out!"

And so it was. Newton's vision cleared enough to see he'd grossly miscalculated. He sank to the deck, forcing a laugh.

"Tomorrow, then."

Old Pete sighed and shook his head. And the drinking game continued.

But Newton sat where he'd crumpled, his head thrown back against the curved planks. Somewhere on the river a ship's messenger rang eight bells. Midnight . . . the larboard watch. Newton closed his eyes, and an image rose in his mind—his father's prized mantel clock . . . the mahogany case and brass hands and symbols—the sun, the ciphers, the child with hourglass in hand. Inscribed around the enameled dial, around the hours marked off with imminent precision, was a Latin expression: "Vulnerant omnes, ultima necat." *All of them wound, the last one kills.*

He used to imagine himself as the child. But tonight he recognized himself as the hourglass, turned by a mysterious and powerful hand, at the mercy of the sand trickling through his narrow neck. His necktie felt tight, and he pulled at it even as he tried to banish the image. But it would not be banished.

*Take heed,* the image seemed to warn, *mortality is at hand.*

# CHAPTER

## ⊰ 16 ⊱

*Royal Artillery Ground, London*
*Late June 1747*

Another fistfight broke out near the knoll, a nobleman wept over his heavy betting losses, three drunken sailors belted out "The Income Tax" song . . . and they had yet to break for lunch. Mary smiled. It was just another day at the cricket field.

She was glad to be part of this diverse and disorderly crowd because cricket allowed Alex to be in London for the Season. The patron sport of the Royal Navy, cricket kept the fickle public interested in their sailors and sanguine toward a war everyone but King George agreed had carried on far too long. As Alex liked to say, the Navy dispensed much worse assignments than team sports during the London Season.

The crowd roared and Mary looked to the field in time to see a white-flanneled batsman, flushed and grinning, score a run.

The Royal Navy had retaken the lead. She scanned the Navy team for Alex, spotting his dark head bobbing amongst the players pounding the shoulders, head, and back of their batsman. She knew he'd be up to bat soon—this was her third match and she had the system down cold.

Dorrie sat next to her on the aisle, humming the catchy tax tune, and Mary's heart caught a little at the thought of leaving her witty cousin. The Season was at an end. The Churchills and the fashionable London crowd would leave next month for Epsom, and Mary Catlett, country cousin, would go home to Chatham, Kent.

But oh, what a Season they had shared. Mary would never forget browsing the brassy, dazzling shops in Cheapside, promenading through St. James' Park, paying the "stairs-foot money" and climbing to St. Paul's dome for the panoramic view. She had discovered the pleasure of circulating libraries, the lure of book clubs, and the fascinating variety of newspapers. The sedan chairs and hackneys and general bedlam of the teeming energetic city were forever etched on her brain.

And accompanying them everywhere was Alex. After the shock of the Easter morning tree encounter had worn off, he'd been more inclined to escort them to the "adventurous" parts of town. With Jack completing the foursome, they'd strolled the pastoral and slightly risqué paths of Vauxhall's pleasure gardens. They participated in choice elements of the May Fair celebrations. Just recently they braved the furor and wickedness surrounding Covent Garden to see David Garrick in his new two-act farce.

It occurred to Mary, with not a little chagrin, she would

have to admit her mother was right—she had desperately needed a change. And the distraction of the London Season had served her well.

Lord Churchill rejoined them, deep in conversation with a rather stern-looking man, his suit of black a somber departure from the collection of pale summer linen splashed about the pavilion. The men settled into seats behind them, Lord Churchill reaching out to squeeze Dorrie's shoulder before asking the man, "And your son?"

The curved bat flashed and Mary, along with a good portion of the crowd, cheered as with a resounding *crack!* the red wooden ball connected and flew through the air.

". . . East India fleet just returned," the man was saying in solemn tones. "I have exhausted my contacts there. But—"

The cheering crowd issued a collective groan as a fielder made a diving catch and struck the batsman out. Enthusiasts of the opposing team applauded and shouted advice to their players as Alex jogged onto the field.

". . . along the Gold Coast. Manesty's had no word from the captain since the *Greyhound* sailed. I fear the worst."

Mary heard the man's grave statement as if from a distance, the smile for Alex frozen on her face. The bookmakers shouted odds, and gamblers bet furiously on the popular Navy captain. The drunken sailors took up "God Save the King," and a host of spectators laughingly joined in with hearty voices.

Mary sat immobile, watching Alex take a stance in front of the wicket, her heart pounding, her mind racing. Could there be more than one Manesty? More than one *Greyhound*?

The bowler's arm drew back, then propelled the ball toward

the wicket. "Send him victorious! Happy and glorious!" warbled the sailors as *crack!* went the bat. The crowd surged to their feet, cheering as Alex ran toward the opposite wicket.

Mary stood with them, watching the players shuffle position, the umpires moving with them, the sun glistening off their bats as Alex skidded to a halt at the wicket, safe. But long after the nonstriker had scored and the crowd had settled, Mary still stood, now facing the men behind her.

Lord Churchill glanced her way, then focused on her face, his own showing alarm and concern. "What is it, child?"

Mary stared hard at the black-clad man who looked back at her with blank eyes.

"You . . . you are . . ."

Dorrie rose up beside her, holding her arm in a fierce grip.

Lord Churchill came to his feet. "Miss Catlett—"

At that the other man stood, a mixed look of astonishment and distress rippling across his face.

Mary blinked. "You are . . . C-Captain Newton."

Out of the corners of her eyes, she saw the Churchills glancing back and forth between her and Newton, troubled with this obvious lack of protocol, struggling to resolve the dilemma.

"I am," the man nodded, then turned to Lord Churchill.

"Forgive me, sir. I knew this lady's family some years past, when she was but a child." Newton attempted a smile. "I believe she was recently . . . acquainted . . . with my son."

Lord Churchill nodded slowly, still frowning.

Newton filled the growing silence. "Perhaps Miss Catlett would take refreshment with me." It was more of a statement than an invitation, and he rushed to petition Mary's patron.

"With your permission, of course."

"Of course." Lord Churchill stepped back, allowing Newton to offer his hand to Mary.

She took his hand and the crowd roared, and it occurred to her somewhere in the back of her mind that Alex had probably just scored a run.

Newton handed her onto the well-trod grass, drawing her away from the pavilion. They moved toward a white canvas tent where champagne corks popped almost continuously and people milled about, talking and laughing.

"A glass of champagne, perhaps?" He gestured toward the tent, but she declined and they walked on along the field.

Newton drew breath to speak several times before he finally cleared his throat.

"Did my son leave you with . . ." He hesitated, seeming to search for the right words. "With an understanding?"

"Yes," she said with conviction, then looked at him, blinking back tears, and whispered, "no." He grimaced and she swallowed through a tight throat.

"Nothing formal . . . not in so many words."

They made a turn and walked on, her hand tucked firmly into the crook of his arm, his hand now covering hers.

"In summer past I received some letters from John—one of them half a year old."

She looked at him and he frowned.

"His situation was . . . quite serious—serious enough to require a rescue."

"And in these letters, there was nothing . . . no word for me?"

Newton drew to a halt. "Miss Catlett," he turned so he was facing her. "You are a remarkable and faithful young woman. If I may speak as a father and be so bold to offer you advice . . ." He sighed and looked out at the field, then back to her. "Lord Clarendon is an honorable man—and an exceptional Navy captain. I know he admires you greatly."

The umpire called "Time" just then, and the masses began to fan out, rushing to secure the perfect spot along the field for a picnic lunch. Mary spotted Dorrie rushing toward them, her face pinched in concern.

"Mr. Newton—"

Newton grasped her upper arms, and she looked into a face stricken with loss.

"John is not coming home, Miss Catlett. I know it in my heart."

She shook her head in denial, and he gripped her arms tighter.

"Your whole life—*this* life"—he waved a hand encompassing the cricket field and the crowds of nattily dressed Londoners—"is in front of you. Please, *please* do not squander it on the dream of a sailor lost at sea."

Dorrie arrived then, flushed and breathless, and Newton bowed to both women, making his departure without another word. Dorrie looked after him a moment, then took Mary's arm and coaxed her back to the pavilion.

"Strawberries and cream," she declared. "Everything improves with strawberries and cream."

But Mary did not want strawberries and cream. She did not want fancy sandwiches and delicate pastries on exquisite china.

She shook her head. *No more,* she thought. No more chocolates and rare teas. No more coffees and parlor games and hands of whist. No more color and lights and personalities surging toward her from every side. The Season was over, and Mary had engaged in so much pretext and amusement that she felt her life had become an elaborate masquerade.

She did not want any more London extravagance.

Alex walked toward them, his flannel suit wrinkled and grass-stained, a happy smile on his tanned face . . . until he saw Mary's. He lengthened his stride and was at her side in moments, taking her hand in his, frowning down at its coldness.

He sent Dorrie to her father, then pulled Mary aside and studied her.

"What is it?"

She looked into his green eyes and was reminded of her mother's prized candy dish of emerald glass. And how it only made an appearance for special occasions because George loved candy and would leave the intricate top too close to the table's edge. Her chest began to heave with the memory of the parlor and John's lingering presence, and she clamped her jaw to keep from bursting into sobs right there on the grass.

"Tell me," Alex pressed. "Tell me what I can do."

"Take me to Chatham," she said through an aching throat. "I want to go home."

# PART III

*You know who a person really is*
*by the language they cry in.*

— MENDE PROVERB

# CHAPTER

## ⊸ 17 ⊷

T he mood on deck was eerie.

Almost as soon as the *Greyhound* had dropped anchor early afternoon, a chilly fog—"thick enough to stand on," claimed Old Pete—rolled onto the banks and bound every ship to her spot. And then the tales and superstitions began. Legends of ships that collect lifeless sailors and rumors of souls passing over the Brig of the Dead had the men carrying salt in their pockets to keep ghosts at bay.

And the captain was no better, Newton thought.

Gother found it "passin' strange" that his sailors did nothing more than drop a net in the shallow water to draw up bucking, flipping cod, four and five feet long, their bellies flashing silver in the mist. When the Portuguese crew pulled in the first monstrous fish, Gother slapped Jack Celso on the back and declared, " 'Ee's a jammer!" But after the fourth and fifth haul, the fish coming in faster than the crew could gut and salt them, Gother wondered aloud if they'd come upon luck of another, more ominous, kind. And then he'd stared pointedly at Newton.

The captain had taken to blaming every problem, every snapped line or unexplained mishap, on the passenger who dared to mock God. Never mind that the ship had suffered from a year of sailing close to the equator, wearing ragged in the blistering heat. Never mind that even as they'd left the mountainous coast of Annobon and crossed the Atlantic to Brazil, the sails and cordage strained from heavy wear. In Gother's superstitious mind, myth was stronger than reason.

But Newton felt unsettled for reasons that had nothing to do with the mysteries of fog or fish. As they'd sailed north from Brazil, meandering with the pull of the North Atlantic Drift, he'd carelessly picked up one of the few books onboard—an English translation of *The Imitation of Christ* by Thomas à Kempis. It was the title that had intrigued him. He'd weighed the book in his hand, recalling his conversation with the African chief's daughter more than a year past.

*"So you cannot imagine,"* she'd asked, *"a life lived as the Jesuits recommend—in imitation of Christ?"*

He did not then, and he could not now. But his indifference toward the idea had shifted to unease as he'd read passage after passage in the little devotional.

*Vanity of vanities!* the first chapter had begun. *All is vanity, except our loving God and serving only Him.* Vanity to seek riches, vanity to follow the desires of the flesh, vanity to think only of this present life. Newton had never thought himself vain. But the Dutch monk who'd written that passage would find him so.

He shook those thoughts free as he cast his net over the *Greyhound*'s side. He stared into the frigid shallows, marveling as a massive cod swam right into the trap, its brown and green dorsal twisting lazily as it nosed about for an opening. Newton tightened the noose, and his mother's voice eased into his head.

*"Follow me, and I will make you fishers of men."* The words of Jesus, spoken to brothers as they fished in the Sea of Galilee. An invitation and a ready acceptance. The clarity of his mother's tender voice startled him, and he dropped the edge of the net, letting the cod swim free.

The Portuguese sailors laughed, taunting him in their rapid-fire language, their breaths puffing into the frosty air as they hauled another fish over the side. Newton closed his mind to the book and his mother's voice, and forced a grin as he adjusted the net and waited for the next unwary cod.

The afternoon passed leisurely as the crew moved from station to station—casting nets at the rail, layering the expertly filleted cod in wooden barrels under Old Barley's watchful eye, collecting seawater for the brine, carting the sealed casks below deck. Gother's tomcat reclined on the smooth deck, picking over whatever Old Barley threw its way. And all the while Newton forced himself to laugh with the crew, even as the little devotional book called to him.

By late afternoon a hard gale blew in from the west, stirring the vapor and pushing patches of slushy slob ice against the ship. The fog lifted and the captain, itching to leave the banks before sunset, directed his crew to store the remaining cod and stand by to cast off.

Against a sky of reds and oranges, the crew worked in well-trained unison, hauling on the halyards until the canvas sails stretched tightly to the top of the masts. As the sails rose, Gother gave the second command.

"Anchors aweigh!"

The command passed forward to Jackson, the first mate, who passed it along to the men on the forecastle head, working the capstan to hoist and heave the anchor. The men strained as they pushed the horizontal bars of the capstan until the anchor was up and locked into place. The sails quickly filled, and the ship began to pick her way to the open sea.

"First mate!" Gother called.

"Aye, Captain!"

"Set course for Liverpool!" And a cheer went up from the homesick crew.

The *Greyhound* bustled with activity—the Portuguese climbing rope ladders to go aloft and adjust sails, Jackson giving and taking orders, the older men coiling ropes and securing lines. Newton, glad to fish but unwilling as a passenger to crew, stood on the quarterdeck, watching the island's bedrock cliffs fade with the setting sun.

Newton frowned. It should have been a happy moment a full year after leaving McCraig and his life on the Guinea coast, finally, *finally* taking the trade winds east and going home—home to his motherland and familiarity and Mary. But lingering, constantly leaning, tapping on his brain, were the Dutch monk's words.

It was not the man's warnings to *fear* God, who sits in judgment, that troubled him. For even Virgil acknowledged there is a God who is mindful of right and wrong. It was more the monk's dire prediction of man's chosen path—his impenitence, his spiritual rejection, leaving him permanently out of favor with Almighty God.

And in pondering these beliefs somewhere deep in his mind, a question formed: *What if these things are true?* What if his profanity, his indifference, his pursuit of pleasure left him not only disgraced but bound for hell?

An iceberg—beautiful and dangerous—loomed close off the starboard side, reflecting the sun's dying rays. *Doomed,* he thought, staring at the glittering mass. He was as doomed as the next unwary ship to encounter that ice. Except he had set his own course in life without the least concern for the consequences.

He stood on the deck, waiting for his former harmony, waiting for something to change the shock of this revelation. He waited through the sunset in the bite of the bitter winter wind until the mountains of Newfoundland were gone from the horizon, until the aurora borealis danced red, green, and blue in the northern sky. And then he climbed down the companionway to his cabin, shivering, his spirit in complete chaos.

*There is no peace unto the wicked,* Kempis had written, quoting the words of the biblical God. *On that,* Newton thought, *we all can heartily agree.*

# CHAPTER

## ⊰ 18 ⊱

*The North Atlantic*
*3:00 A.M., March 10, 1748*

Newton sat bolt upright, gasping with shock. He was half out of bed, groping beside his cot for flint to light the lantern when the second gush of frigid water doused him.

The ship rolled, throwing him onto the floor. Wet. At least an inch of water sloshed about the cabin. He looked up and saw only flashing sky where planking should be. He crawled back, feeling for his clothes, finding the soggy mass on the floor where he'd discarded them. He cursed and struggled into the sodden breeches, his fingers fighting the slippery buttons.

And then a *crack!* and an anguished groan from above stopped him cold. Only one object could make that horrific of a sound. A mast was splintering in two.

The reaction was instantaneous. Amidst the scream of tearing wood came panicked cries from the deck. The ship was sinking.

Newton threw on his jacket, stepped into a boot, tore it off and poured the seawater out of it, then jammed it on again. He was out of the cabin and halfway up the hatchway when Gother shouted to him from below.

"Git back ta tha cabin and find me a blade!"

Newton obeyed, leaping from the fifth step as Jack Celso scrambled up in his place. He hit the deck hard and glanced up in time to watch Celso step through the hatch only to be swept up by a wall of water and, illuminated by a series of lightning flashes, tossed into the roiling sea.

Newton stared up, mute, his mouth hanging open. That would have been him at the hatch, swept into the sea, if not for the captain's command.

"Go!" the captain shouted.

Newton's mind snapped back to his mission. A blade. He needed to find a blade.

He tore back to the cabin, dizzy with the first threads of fear. He careened about the room as the ship pitched and yawed and water poured through the ceiling. Where was Gother's knife? He fumbled around the captain's desk, seeing in his mind's eye the black horn handle, slightly curved before the small brass guard . . . the long, straight blade and upsweeping cutting edge—his hand brushed against a hard leather sheath, and he felt a moment of victory before he was thrown to the floor, the knife gripped in his outstretched hand.

He crawled through the water to the doorway, then pulled

himself up as the ship plunged downward. He stumbled through the wardroom, hearing the frantic squeals and squawks and bleats of the livestock between decks as he struggled up the same hatchway that had claimed Jack Celso minutes ago. He eased open the hatch with that horrific scene playing over in his mind and immediately replaced it with the reality on deck.

Lightning flashed all around the ship, revealing wave after wave crashing against and over the bulwark. Rain fell in torrents, lashing at the crews' bent backs even as dead water ran across the forecastle, slapping them, as the ship rolled side to side.

Newton climbed out and closed the hatch, gripping the handle in one hand, the captain's blade in the other. He looked aft and spied Jackson, alone on the quarterdeck, manhandling the wheel. He followed the line of the mainmast up into the angry sky. Sails and rigging flapped wildly in the gale-force winds, but it looked sound.

His gaze snapped toward the forecastle at a sudden scream. The top of the broken foremast swung violently as the ship yawed, flinging a man in the riggings like a rag doll. The crew sawed at the lines, trying to free both the mast and the man. Newton gripped the knife and made a run for it. He made the half deck before the wind drove the ship helplessly into a trough. She heaved and rocked heavily.

He clung to the rail and looked down. The sea was in absolute chaos. Large waves came from every direction, colliding with one another to form massive waves that dipped and swelled and slammed against the side of the *Greyhound*. From what he could see, their little two-masted, eighty-ton vessel was afloat only at the whim of plunging mountains of gray water. He closed his eyes and mouthed the words of Dante—*"Abandon hope, all ye who enter here."*

---

*Dawn*

Newton worked the foot pump in earnest, glad to have a task that would drive the blood through his frozen veins and generate some heat. The wind had dropped, but the rain still beat against the crew as they pumped and bailed the water from the damaged ship.

Every man not at the pumps was set to gathering clothing and bedding, plugging the holes and gaps as the *Greyhound* continued to take on water. Old Pete, master carpenter, followed behind, nailing ragged pieces of timber over the bungholes, muttering Irish blessings.

Newton took stock: A large portion of the foremast—gone. The upper timbers on the starboard side—gone. Warm meals, warm grog, warm blankets for sleeping—gone.

They'd managed to cut down Galego from the foremast, but he'd been so shaken, the captain had sent him to the sailmaker's loft to stitch up what canvas they had salvaged. The sails were badly damaged and still flapped about at the highest points. The large fly-by-night was rent in two when the mast shattered. They were in a bad way, Newton acknowledged. But they were alive.

A stifled sob broke into his thoughts, and he looked across the pump to Paiva, the Portuguese cooper. Paiva's foot worked the pump, but he hugged his thin arms to his body, his shoulders shaking. Newton considered the boy—a man, really, at twenty—and clapped his hands together, rubbing them. He and the cooper had spent many days together, trading languages as Paiva repaired barrels.

"In a few days, my friend," Newton began, forcing the man to meet his eye, "this distress will serve for a subject over a glass of wine."

"No." The word came out like a bark, the young sailor shaking his head, his tears blending with the freezing rain. "Celso . . . Celso . . ." Paiva shuddered with grief. "Está . . . Está tarde demais agora." *It is too late now.*

Newton opened his mouth, then closed it, frowning, and silently amended his list. Jack Celso, carpenter's mate—gone.

—  ———

10:00 A.M.

Newton fought the complicated knots with fingers frozen nearly stiff. He'd been roped to the mainmast for an hour, working the pump as the gale-force winds returned and battered the ship in another round of punishing waves and driving rain. He had to get out of the elements, even for just a moment.

Jackson stepped up, working the knots until they pulled free. Newton dropped to his hands and knees, his teeth chattering too hard to thank the first mate as he crawled toward the hatchway. With his last ounce of energy, he pulled open the hatch, slipped inside, and let it bang closed after him.

It seemed so still on the steps. He would have stayed right there had the ship stopped lurching to and fro, threatening to throw him to the floor. He climbed to the deck and stood there, wondering if he would ever be warm again, when the captain burst from the wardroom. Gother paused for a moment, glaring at Newton, before growling out an order.

"Follow me."

Newton slogged after the captain, following him down the runged ladder and into the bowels of the vessel, past the sailmaker's loft where they collected Galego, past the crew's quarters where hammocks no longer hung, and onto the deck above the fore-cargo hold. They squatted around the hatch's coaming, Newton and Galego brushing away rain as it splashed onto their hatless heads.

"If we dunt adjust the ballast, we'll be sunk."

Newton frowned down at the hatch. Surely Gother did not mean to send them into the hold in this violent weather. He shook his head. "Why not scrap the canons and shot?"

Gother glared at him. "We done 'at the first go 'roun smornen." They locked eyes, and Gother continued.

"Any rate, I 'spect the cargo's the only fing keepin' us afloat. But I needs the heavy fings moved leeward—git the damaged side higher in the water."

Galego was nodding, but Newton was reviewing the cargo— beeswax, ivory, a little gold, and cords of camwood for dye and dunnage.

"The ivory's 'eaviest, then the wood. Shift it all leeward." Gother stared at Newton. " 'less you can fink of anudder way to save us . . . Mr. Newton."

The ship groaned as she fought the punishing elements, her

plating pulsing from the water pressure. Newton stared back, too tired and cold to argue.

"Well, then, less git this cover off."

All three of the men strained to loosen the tightly sealed cover, but the weather seemed to have frozen it in place. Then, the very moment Newton thought it hopeless, the cover turned, and they lifted it away. There arose a warm and inviting fragrance of lumber and honeycomb, and Newton found himself looking forward to this dangerous mission.

Gother broke a cardinal rule and lit a lantern, then lowered it as far as he could into the hold. After a moment he nodded and turned to Galego.

"Gwahn en." Both he and Newton grabbed an arm, Gother calling encouragement as they lowered the man into the pitch-black hold. "Assit. Down ya go."

Galego hit the floor with an encouraging shout, and Gother handed down the lantern. Newton followed and soon stood in the aromatic hold, looking up.

"I'll be sealin' yer in. Don' waste the lamp."

The hatch slammed closed, and the men looked at each other for a moment, then at their immediate surroundings. The ship continued to pitch and yaw, but the cargo remained, for the most part, precisely where they'd stowed it weeks ago. Their final trade—walrus tusk from the Hudson Bay—still lay on the shelves in front of them, anchored into place with the shrubby branchlets of the camwood tree. Here and there a piece of wood or a jute sack of beeswax had tumbled to the floor, but the damage was minor compared to that above deck.

By mutual consent the men made their way starboard,

squeezing through the tight aisles to retrieve the hard ivory, Newton gingerly holding the swaying lantern before him—they were surrounded by dry wood, and a fire in the hold would be certain death. They came upon the mass of creamy incisors and worked out a method in which they would carry the seventy-pound tusks over the shoulder and under the arm, making a circular route starboard to leeward.

They loaded up and set off, only to be thrown hard against the dunnage as the ship rolled viciously.

Newton kept his eye on the swinging lantern, sweating for the first time in weeks and crying out, "If this will not do, the Lord have mercy upon us!"

It was an offhand statement, and Galego simply grunted. But Newton was instantly struck by the words—sincere words—bursting from lips that had done nothing but blaspheme God for years. Mercy? What did he know of mercy?

*Nothing,* his mind answered, and the sweat chilled on his frame. *Absolutely nothing.*

------------

*Noon*

Newton crumpled onto his bunk, a half-eaten sea biscuit in his hand.

When Cook and Old Barley had pulled him from the hold, the looks on their faces grim, he knew without being told that the *Greyhound* was going down. He hung his head at the hatch, soaked through in moments, and trudged back to his cabin, numb with cold and exhausted to the point of collapse.

He lay on his cot, seawater dripping onto him through the repaired ceiling, and admitted defeat. He was going to die in the relentless, icy Atlantic, two thousand miles from home, twenty-two years old, and nothing—*nothing*—to show for it. Anxiety nearly strangled the breath from him. It was not so much the plunge into the sea he dreaded. It was knowing, with certainty, that he would die alone, without pity and without God's love and grace.

That knowledge had come to him in slow degrees. Kempis was right. Watts, Onya, his mother—all were right. He had heard but had not wanted to listen.

He closed his eyes and must have dozed because the gruff voice charging into his brain made his ears buzz and skin tingle in alarm.

"Newton!"

He rose on one elbow and stared blearily at Jackson.

"The captain commands you to take the helm."

---

4:00 P.M.

The wall of water rose up, taking the *Greyhound* with it, and Newton started the count. *One . . . two . . . three . . . four . . .* Down went the ship, deep into the chasm, then up again, higher than an earl's house. And he started the count again. *One . . . two . . . three . . .*

And all the while the wind shrieked and the rain pelted him as he stood alone on the quarterdeck, lashed to the wheel, obscure and awful lines from learned monks and kings dancing through his head.

*I will laugh at your calamity,* said Wisdom in the Proverbs. *I will mock when your destruction cometh as a whirlwind . . .*

He shook his head at that, and a wave crashed into him with such force that he could not breathe. He released the wheel and fought the sea pouring down on him. He threw his hands over his nose and mouth, but the sheer force of the water knocked them away.

Finally the wave dispersed, and he gasped great breaths of air, almost as if he had surfaced from the deep. Bitter tears mixed with the rain as he choked on the seawater and his own despair.

*What kind of life is this,* asked Kempis, *where miseries and afflictions are never lacking . . .* Newton steered the ship into the wind and considered that question. And for the first time in his short life, tears streaming down his battered cheeks, he faced the realities of his past.

Oh, he had suffered miseries and afflictions, but he had likewise experienced extraordinary deliverances—none of which were of his own design. He saw that now. And what had been his response to each rescue? Decadence. Insolence. Profane ridicule.

He looked deep into his black heart and thought there had not likely been—nor could there ever be—a reprobate, a sinner, such as John Newton. So there was no escaping his fate, and the elements all around the *Greyhound* seemed to confirm it. The wind and rain were almost surreal, everything boiling together in an eerie half-light . . . no up and down, no starboard or port. He faced the nightmare and suddenly wished to know the worst.

A rogue wave appeared out of nowhere, and Newton looked up at the crest sixty feet above him. The wave hesitated, then hit, rolling the ship almost entirely on her side.

The lee rail disappeared under the rushing water, and Newton hugged the helm, his body hanging by the ropes in midair. The ship's list was so severe the frothing sea slapped at the fife rails around the masts and surged down the hatchways. She stood on her beam ends, groaning with the stress of trying to right herself, and hung for a moment, neither capsizing nor righting.

Newton stared down into the roiling green water . . . stared deep into the yawning mouth of death.

"God help us," he whispered, and let the wheel run free.

# CHAPTER

## 19

*Lloyd's Coffee House, London*
*March 1748*

The two captains stared at each other across the polished table, the racket in the place forcing them to lean in to hear and be heard.

"You've given up the *Greyhound* for . . . lost . . . then."

Manesty studied the man who spoke with such tightly controlled emotion—or attempted to . . . his voice quavered on the word *lost*, and he turned the tea mug round and round in his hands. Manesty shook his head.

"No. Not yet. I only tell you I've had no word of them—neither from Gother himself, nor from other vessels on that route."

"And the Marine?"

"The Marine continues to press for information from the

Admiralty. But their interest is nominal. John is no longer their concern."

Newton, the accountable father, flinched at that, and Manesty chastised himself for diminishing the son's importance. He rushed to present better scenarios.

"They may have wintered in the Americas, or Gother may not have found him and simply wants to avoid my displeasure."

"If Gother did not find him, he is surely dead."

The finality in the man's words was breathtaking. His air of severity sucked the life out of the coffeehouse atmosphere, leaving the cigar smoke suddenly bitter, the laughter cruel. Manesty shook his head so violently he sent his wig askew.

"You cannot wish it so!"

"I would rather know than wonder, always wonder . . ." Newton's mouth settled into a grim line. "I daresay most men would be of the same mind."

"But there is no hope in knowing."

"There is no solace in hope."

Manesty opened his mouth to refute that but closed it just as abruptly. This was the detached Newton—the man who hid behind arrogance and logic to forestall regret . . . and pity.

A kidney raced by, sliding bowls of sherbet in front of the men. Newton stared down at his, but Manesty picked up his spoon, desperate for a task to fill the yawning silence. Cold radiated from the sherbet and its icy bowl. Even the spoon was frigid. He was so tired of the cold, of winter. No wonder the traders were so hostile, what with—

He looked up at Newton, the situation becoming ever clear.

The man had suffered all he could, and he'd found a way to bring his anguish to an end.

"You've accepted the post, then."

Newton nodded, staring blindly at his bowl and spoon. Manesty carefully placed his own spoon on the shiny table.

"When do you leave?"

"The end of April. When the ice no longer threatens."

Three years as governor of Fort York—collecting fur, defending Hudson Bay, keeping the French at a distance. It was a worthy position. And it was remote . . . like the man.

Newton cleared his throat. "I . . . delayed for as long as I could. I had ho—" He cleared his throat again. "I had . . . thought . . . John could accompany me." He shook his head and took a deep, steadying breath. "But no more. No more."

Manesty ached for the man—for his loss of hope, for his utter despair. He thought perhaps fathering the son had been the greatest failure of Newton's life. And he had no way of putting it to right.

They sat together, neither speaking, the lively atmosphere— the shouted news reports and calls for lotteries, the smells of roasted beef and brewing coffee—in complete contrast to their solemnity.

At length Newton pushed back from the table. "You will see the Marine again?"

"Tomorrow."

"And he remains in contact with Miss Catlett?"

Manesty inclined his head, wondering at this line of questioning.

Newton hesitated, then pulled a small packet of letters from his inside pocket. Manesty recognized the smudged writing on the envelope, yellowed from two years of wear. Inside were agonizing, pleading words from a desolate young man. Newton removed the sheets with a delicate hand, and Manesty noted the fraying crease and edges—evidence of much study . . . evidence of a father longing for a son.

Newton separated several sheets from the others, folded them, and passed them across the table. Manesty raised a brow and Newton frowned.

"Letters from John to Miss Catlett."

Manesty looked from the table to his friend and shook his head. "Why?"

"I fear she will not accept Lord Clarendon until she knows the truth of John's . . . enslavement and suffering—that he cannot have survived it these past two years."

Manesty laid his hand atop the letters, struggling with his friend's logic and his urge to shield the woman from further pain.

Newton pushed to his feet and held out his hand. "Goodbye, my friend."

Manesty stood and shook the hand, sensing somewhere deep in his chest that this was a final good-bye. Many poignant phrases flashed in his mind, but he discarded them one by one until Newton had donned his hat and coat and, without another word, was gone.

Manesty sank into his chair and reached for the letters. By habit he began reading. *My dear Miss Catlett,* the first letter began. *The hope of you is all that I have left within me.* He folded the letters closed, mortified at his own intrusion and surprised at the tears that bald declaration had brought to his eyes.

*"There is no solace in hope,"* Newton had argued. Perhaps he was right . . . perhaps he was right.

# CHAPTER

## ❧ 20 ❧

*Somewhere in the North Atlantic*
*Dawn, March 11*

T he *Greyhound* was a floating ruin.

The sun that rose on a calm sea revealed sails and rigging torn to tatters, the topmast shot away, and scarcely a solid length of rope left to secure anything. The ship heeled heavily to port, forcing the shredded starboard side up and out of the water. What remained of the sails puffed in fits and starts, advancing the vessel at a crawl.

The storm had finally blown itself out, but it had taken the *Greyhound*'s sailing ability with it.

Newton shivered on the quarterdeck with the captain and crew, watching the sun's bright rays caress the empty ocean as he half listened to Gother's report. They'd been blown off course— how far north or south of the fifty-first parallel was any man's guess. They were steering toward what Jackson hoped was Ireland, no more than three hundred miles due east from his best calculations. Their victuals were sparse, the casks of grain and meat and vegetables smashed in the hold, the livestock washed away. What remained—fresh water, some pulse for the hogs, and the salted cod from the Grand Banks—would last them little more than a week.

The situation was bad, Gother acknowledged, but not desperate. Not yet.

Newton heard it all, his empty stomach rumbling in protest, his mind still resting on that moment he'd stared death in the face, petitioned God for help . . . and got it. The ship should have capsized. They should all be at the bottom of the ocean now. But God had heard him—*him* . . . the scoffer, the blasphemer.

"Fortune favors the brave," Gother was saying.

*Perhaps . . . perhaps . . .* Newton thought. But now, half a day later, he supposed it more likely the apostle Paul spoke true when he asked Christians everywhere: "If God be for us, who can be against us?"

---

*Dawn, March 15*

A single word launched Newton out of his cold, hard, pillowless bunk. Shouted joyfully from the watch on the forecastle, it traveled mouth to mouth, stem to stern, until the cry reverberated through the quarterdeck's planks over his head.

"Land!"

He hit the floor fully dressed. The clothing on their backs was the only material the crew retained after the frantic effort to stop the ship's leaking gaps in the storm. And not one of the men had been warm since.

He leapt up the hatchway and joined the crew on the fore-castle, his breath puffing out in great clouds, his spirit marveling at the red ball of sun as it crept over the horizon, casting the distant coast in brilliant scarlet and blinding oyster white. They were saved, was the happy chant. They were home.

They looked to be about twenty miles off northwest Ire-land—twenty miles to steaming bowls of *ballymaloe* and roaring fires . . . twenty miles to shelter and plenty. And Newton recalled the boy, the blissful, big-eyed child he'd been, stumbling up the Old Wapping Stairs and skipping down Red Lyon Street to the little house, to his mother's embrace. Faith had been so simple then—faith in kind words and gentle hands . . . and the assurance of home. He blinked back tears that seemed to spring up so easily now.

The captain stepped into their midst, his back to the moun-tainous coast. He held up a pint of brandy—all that remained to warm them as the *Greyhound* limped to shore.

"Hie yerselves below and git yer cups. We'll have a toast."

The sailors were gone and back in a thrice, holding out their cups with filthy scarred hands. The captain doled out the liquor, and Cook handed over the last of the bread made from the coarse pulse. Gother raised his cup.

"May God hold you in the hollow of his hand."

"Amen" in several languages greeted that sentiment, and the crew inhaled the fare, balancing themselves on the sloping deck.

Congratulations passed back and forth . . . a celebration of survival.

They began to talk of what they would do when they made shore, most of the discussion involving warm fires and vast amounts of food. Old Pete thought he'd stuff himself on white pudding sausage and sleep a full week. Paiva spoke dreamily of cakes and scones—confections of gingerbread and strawberry and raisin.

"I wish it might prove land at last."

Every head turned and every eye narrowed at the first mate with his dire assertion and grave tone. Jackson stood apart from the group, squinting at the coast and shaking his head.

A hot debate ensued, Old Barley arguing for the promised land, outlining the mainland with his stubby fingers, circling the small islands with a flourish. But within minutes the sun rose full, and the "islands" began to flame red. In half an hour the "coastline," proving to be nothing but an artful collection of clouds, vanished into the horizon. And with it, the crew's hopes, their glow of reprieve, vanished too.

They were adrift somewhere on the open North Sea in a flat calm on a wrecked ship with little clothing and even less food. In a week they'd be as good as dead.

----

*March 16–30*

The gale struck from the southeast this time, battering the broken ship and forcing the crew back to the pumps.

For hours on end the men labored on deck, their bodies

wracked with shivers from the bitter winds, their stomachs cramped with hunger. At noon Cook would divide half a salted cod between ten sailors, fresh water their only other sustenance.

The captain sailed the *Greyhound* with the wind on her damaged side, navigating by guess and by God as the storm pushed them farther and farther north. And all the while he hounded Newton, blaming him for their misfortune. He interrupted Newton's sleep, his reading, and even his efforts at the pumps, calling him a "Jonah," urging the crew to cast lots against the man who dared to mock God.

"Repent! Repent!" Gother shouted at his unwelcome passenger. And the crew would turn away, frowning in unease.

But Newton did not need a storm or the captain's reproach to prick his conscience. When his strength was spent and hunger kept him from sleeping, he lost himself in reading Kempis. And the words in the little book confirmed Newton's greatest fear: he had, at last, been found out by the powerful hand of God.

Tallow they had aplenty, and he burned it with abandon, devouring the monk's words. *Wherever you are, and wheresoever you turn,* Kempis wrote, *you are wretched unless you turn to God.* Wretched . . . he was certainly wretched. Slow tears ran down his cheeks as he considered his offenses, one by one, and received his judgment—*guilty, guilty, guilty.* And though he confessed them all, he could not be unburdened. In desperation he quoted the Twenty-fifth Psalm—*The troubles of my heart are enlarged: O bring me out of my distresses.* But there was no redemption.

On deck, the incessant pumping to keep the ship above water took its toll. Whether from hunger or exhaustion or defeat, Old Barley collapsed and could not be revived. Almost immediately the wind shifted, blowing gently for the first time in a fortnight. They released the sailmaker to the sea, fearing the prospect of feeding on his flesh should starvation destroy their minds.

As Galego pushed the wasted body through the portal, Gother stared hard at Newton. "That shoulda been you."

Newton nodded, his tears freezing, thick and salty, as they fell. And the *Greyhound* drifted onward: eight crew, one Jonah.

———

*April 7*

The word spread with less confidence this time.

The men hovered on the forecastle, staring to the east, silently contemplating what appeared to be an island of towering cliffs. The very last of their cod awaited them, but they refused to a man to eat. It would be an act of surrender.

A growl and a *splash!* drew their eyes portside. Floating next to the *Greyhound*, their black-and-white dress giving them the look of small friars, was a pair of puffins. The seabirds stared back at the men, blinking in open curiosity.

And then a shout broke the silence. Birds meant land, and land meant rescue.

Grateful tears burst from hardened sailors, and when the cheering stopped and the cod was distributed, the speculation began. How far north had they drifted? Had they made the western isles of Scotland? The bitter March wind cut through their ragged clothing, yet they refused to leave the deck.

By minute degrees the shoreline revealed itself. Mossy green cliffs and red rock loomed before them, and the decision was unanimous. Dead ahead was the island of Tory, on the north coast of Ireland.

Dead ahead, two hundred miles from Liverpool and a single day from abject despair, was home.

# CHAPTER

## ⊰ 21 ⊱

*Londonderry, Ireland*
*April 1748*

I *nfidel.*
It was a name he would have proudly answered to not long ago when his greatest dilemma was how to entertain himself of an evening. Like the biblical Saul of Tarsus, Newton had made religious scoffing and persecution an art form, and he was seldom without a target.

But the past four weeks in the Atlantic had revealed to him something about faith. He did not understand it, but he knew intrinsically that without faith, without trust and hope, his life would be dominated by doubt . . . his life would be black with unfathomable despair.

And so every day, whilst the *Greyhound* gained repair, from the ringing of the nine-o'clock morning bells to the nine peals of evening curfew, he walked the steep, narrow streets of the hillside town, thinking . . . thinking . . . He followed the massive stone walls that had fortified this city against siege and attack . . . and considered the walls he'd so carefully, meticulously built around his heart. He encountered the spiny gorse with its gold blossoms that smelled like sweet coconut . . . and thought of Plaintain Island and Pey Ey, and how he'd been brought safely through that threat and so many other dangers. He passed the same street fiddler, playing yet another melancholy air . . . and thought of the Guinea captives and their mournful songs.

Eventually, inevitably, he'd find himself on London Street at the doors of St. Columb's Cathedral, the old stone pillars and arches calling to him. *Come to me . . . come to me . . .*

And he would enter and walk the aisles, climb to the galleries and run his hand along the oak banister, praying. But his prayer was like the cry of the ravens—the sound harsh and hungry. There was no mother now to feed him the catechisms and proofs, no biscuits and crackling fire to nurture him as he memorized hymns and poems. And the ache for that time washed over him upon every visit. But still he came.

It was there, in the nave of the cathedral, that Newton had his epiphany. For days on end he sat in the white square pews and studied the Scriptures until he discovered the captain had, indeed, been right—Newton had been a Jonah. He had run from God instead of trusting Him. He had wanted his own way, and his defiance had wounded those around him.

But even more than a Jonah, Newton saw himself in the New Testament as the Prodigal. Just like that wasteful son,

Newton had engaged in riotous living, had been starved and humiliated in a foreign country, and had suddenly decided to make his way home.

Both men in the Scriptures discovered almost too late that no failing was too great, no dilemma too difficult for God. And when they came to their senses, when they were obedient, they discovered God's mercy and grace had been waiting for them— just for the asking—all along.

Newton closed the Holy Book and looked straight ahead, up the aisle, past the lectern, and into the chancel where the great wooden cross hung. Kempis had much to say about that cross.

*In the Cross is health . . .* he had written. *In the Cross is life; in the Cross is the fullness of heavenly sweetness; in the Cross is strength of mind, joy of spirit, height of virtue, full perfection of all holiness, and there is no help for the soul, or hope of everlasting life, save through the virtue of the Cross.*

The cross. The great organ pipes were silent, but Newton heard the music anyway . . . the melody of Isaac Watts, the great preacher and poet from his childhood. It was as if Watts stood on the chancel and asked:

*Alas, and did my Savior bleed?*
*And did my Sov'reign die?*
*Would he devote that sacred head*
*For such a one as I?*

"Yes." Newton's voice echoed in the empty nave. He said it again, louder. "Yes!"

And like the Prodigal, he got up and walked that long empty path. He approached with not a little worry, uncertain about what awaited him there—anger . . . rejection . . . clemency.

But in the end he needn't have worried. Though he'd spent his entire life running from mercy, in the end, just like the Prodigal's father, mercy came running to him.

# CHAPTER
## 22

Chatham, Kent
April 1748

T he Marine slammed another crate onto the table, muttering darkly.

As he stomped back out the kitchen door, Mary raised an
auburn brow and shot Alex a look that said, *What* is the trouble?
Alex frowned and shrugged, leaving the unspoken question dan-
gling in the spring air between them.

They sat at the worktable surrounded by stacks of crates—
plunder from the Marine's recent trip to the London docks.
Mary had dared to open the first such crate, discovering dried
bunches of what she assumed were indigenous herbs from the
colonies. But she'd no more than sniffed one strong-smelling
bundle before it was snatched from her hand and tossed back

into the crate, followed by a string of curses. The Marine was in a foul mood, no question.

He'd fetched her from her front parlor where Alex had just begun reading to her from *Poor Richard's Almanack*, delighting her with Franklin's colonial wit and wisdom. The Marine had looked from Mary to Alex, and back to Mary again before gruffly requesting their assistance. Of course, any "request" from his lips was, in essence, a command, so they'd jumped to do his bidding and now sat at his table, idle, enduring his temper as they chatted of Benjamin Franklin.

And how she loved to chat with Alex. The longings of the past year had been covered up with so much witty conversation and thoughtful debate, she wondered whatever she'd talked about for the previous eighteen years. He'd told her of his childhood on the rocky coast of Exmoor—of his parents' terraced house on the steep cobbled lane, of his father's premature death and his mother's slow recovery. And they'd debated the significance of a strong male influence on children. She'd confessed her need for adventure—the adrenaline rush of late-night exploits, the thrill of a direct hit from pistol or knife. And they'd laughed many times about their first meeting . . . one of Alex's fondest memories, he said. Even Samson had warmed to their camaraderie, more often than not settling his enormous frame next to her, staring up with adoring eyes as she smoothed his brindled coat.

Yes, life with Alex had become unexpectedly dear. And she wondered for not the first time what their future might hold. Would a marriage between them work? She esteemed him, no doubt. But could she love him—as her mother so clearly loved her father? Would he marry, then desert her—go off to fight yet another of King George's wars, leaving her alone and anxious? And could she really be a viscountess—live within all the formality and responsibility essential to the peerage? These were the questions that surprised her late at night when they drifted into her groggy mind.

But for now, Mary smiled across the table at Alex, her favorite friend, as he regaled her with tales of "electric parties" in London, hosted by Peter Collinson, Franklin's British contemporary. Alex had not attended such a party, he admitted, his green eyes sparkling. But he'd heard breathless stories of toy figures dancing and bells ringing from Collinson's electrical "charge."

"Genius," the Marine mumbled as he kicked a crate under the table. Mary and Alex cut their eyes toward him and he scowled back at them.

"Franklin," he all but shouted. "The man's a diplomatic genius."

Alex waited a beat, then rejoined in all seriousness.

"I understand he's also a bit of a ladies' man."

Mary nodded. "And a *bon vivant*, to be sure."

The Marine threw up his hands in disgust and stomped back into the courtyard.

Mary grinned at Alex and was rewarded with a slow wink. They smiled at each other until Alex leaned back in his chair, drumming his fingers on the table, squinting at her in that familiar thoughtful way.

"Was it not Franklin who coined the phrase—how does it go . . . 'Three may keep a secret . . .'?"

"'If two of them are dead!'" Mary finished for him. They chuckled and Mary continued the game.

"I believe Franklin also said, 'To err is human' . . ."

Alex raised a black brow. "'To repent, divine' . . ."

"'To persist, devilish.'"

"Todd!" The Marine's roar slashed across their *tête-à-tête,* and Alex sighed. He stood and leaned across the table, murmuring, "It must not be too serious . . . he didn't invoke the title."

Mary snorted, then threw her hand across her mouth, somewhat appalled. The viscount was gracious enough to ignore it and retreated to the courtyard.

She watched him go, absently stroking Samson's ears— perked in regular intervals—when the Marine stomped in with another interesting crate. In mere moments Alex returned, a regretful look about him as he pulled on his brown frock coat.

"He says he cannot convince you to work when I am so thoroughly distracting you. So I am banished to run errands."

Mary grimaced. She was quite comfortable, thank you, tucked in by the fire, bantering with Alex. She had not an ounce of desire to do any work.

"Come, Samson."

The mastiff rested his head on Mary's lap, studying his master with sad brown eyes. Alex suppressed a grin and snapped his fingers. "Come." The dog sighed heavily and padded to his master's side, slower than winter molasses.

Alex donned his hat and tweaked the brim. "Miss Catlett."

"Captain Todd."

Man and beast ambled through the courtyard, and she stared after them, wondering how she would endure the Marine's temper alone. She hadn't long to consider that as the man clomped through the door and stood over her, glaring.

"We must speak."

She raised a brow, disliking his brusque tone and menacing stance. Truly, his manners were dreadful. She flicked her hand toward a chair.

"Do sit down. You are hovering."

He shook his head but moved across the room and leaned against the counter, crossing his arms over his chest. He studied her through narrowed eyes.

"What are your intentions toward the viscount?"

She nearly gasped with the man's impertinence and felt a blush creep up her neck.

"*Really,* sir. I fail to see how that is any of your—"

"Do you intend to wed him?"

She was shocked into silence. *Of course* she had asked herself that same question. *Of course* tongues were wagging and the subject was fodder for tea-table discussion. But not even her mother had phrased the question so abruptly. She opened her mouth, trying to suppress her anger.

"Perhaps that is a discussion better suited for you and the viscount."

"Oh, we have discussed it. At length."

At length? Her mind raced. What had they discussed? Her merits? Her demerits? Had the Marine vocally opposed the union? Did Alex think her unfit for the peerage? Even while she searched for a response, the Marine plowed on.

"I told him I have only one reservation. But it is a strong one, and it has a name."

He reached into a drawer, pulled out some folded pages, and threw them onto the table. They skidded halfway across the surface. "John Newton."

Mary stared at the pages, her heart in her throat.

"It seems the father received some letters from the son in '46. Two were addressed to you. He thought it unwise then to forward them." His voice hardened. "I think it unwise still."

The logs settled in the fire behind her, sending up a burst of flame and heat. But Mary felt chilled—right through the bone and into her soul. The contest, the spirit, the very art of conversation was lost to her, but the Marine seemed not to notice and kept speaking.

"I have not read them, though I think it clear the elder Newton has."

She stared at the pages' worn edges but did not touch them. *Why?* her heart cried. *Why has he sent them now?*

The Marine moved into view, his considerable bulk blocking the sunlight from the open door.

"We struck a bargain, you and I, and I have not regretted it until this moment."

He put both hands on the table and leaned forward, his voice firm but soft. "Alexander Todd is one of the finest men I know. He loves you, Mary."

Her head snapped up and she stared into his dark eyes.

"He loves you, and I will not allow you to destroy him. Not if I can stop it. And not over a ghost." He tapped the pages. "Read the letters. Then choose . . . but choose wisely."

He stalked out, leaving the door open.

She stared after him, into the courtyard of afternoon sun,

into a budding spring that was already filling the air with promise. A shaft of light burst through the dusty windowpane and
stabbed at the old and worn sheets of paper. She watched her
hand reach out and settle on them, felt the brittle material, heard
the scratching sound as she dragged the pages closer. She slid her
thumbnail along the edge and spread them open.

*My dear Miss Catlett,* the first letter began. *The hope of you
is all that I have left within me.*

She drew a sharp breath. The words were like a fist to her
heart. She closed her eyes, then forced them back open—forced
herself to read the faded account of a young man succumbing to
heat blisters, starvation, and all manner of suffering. Again and
again she read the words, poetic even in their horrific candor.

The sun was setting, the fire in ashes when she finally folded
the sheets closed and sat hunched in the chair, her head down.
The Marine had not returned, and for that she was unspeakably
thankful.

Many emotions had coursed through her, but the overriding
sentiment—the one that stained her skin and rang in her ears—
was shame. She could not remember a time she had so disappointed herself, and in so doing, failed another. For, ghost or
no, she had failed John Newton. She had stopped praying . . .
stopped hoping. She had simply given up.

She stood, drew on her cloak and gloves, tied on her hat,
and began the walk home. The Marine had done what he
thought was right—he'd forced a choice. And now only time
would prove the wisdom of it.

# CHAPTER

## 23

*Liverpool*
*May 1748*

The *Greyhound* sailed through the mouth of the Pool and raced toward Canning Dock, arriving just before the gates swung closed and trapped ships and water in the innovative wet port. The crew cheered and Newton smiled as the homesick and weary men resumed their chant of "Long live the king!"

They had finally, *finally*, landed on English soil.

Newton stood for the last time on the *Greyhound*'s quarter-deck, overwhelmed with an emotion he was hard-pressed to name. This was the land that had taken the young mother from the child, then betrayed him four years past when he'd been press-ganged onto the *Harwich*. This was the culture that had denied him the principal object of his desire for so, so long. This was the population that had left him to rot on a desert island.

The anguish, the longing, the misery this kingdom had exacted from him was acute. And for that, he was absurdly and profoundly . . . grateful.

He burst out laughing at that insight, startling the cat weaving in and out of his spread legs. He picked up the orange tabby, Gother's replacement for the yellow tom that went missing after the storm. The cat purred against his shirt, echoing the whirr in his own chest—the whirr of a changed heart that could now appreciate the lessons of his wretchedness . . . the whirr of unmitigated hope.

The *Greyhound* eased into the slip, bobbing in the reddish brown water next to vessels of every design and crews of every nationality. From his position Newton could hear shouts in Gaelic, Indian, and Chinese. Off the portside men filled the holds with cotton, guns, and iron, and off the starboard, horses pulled stacks of sugar and cocoa. He was standing at the gateway to the world. But he didn't care.

He dropped the tabby to the deck, picked up his small bundle, and walked the plank to the dock. He was home, and he had a man to thank for that.

------------

*Manesty Lane, Liverpool*

Joseph Manesty sat at his massive oak desk, running his fingers up and down the spiky lavender stems, breathing in the subtle musky fragrance. How he loved his lavender bushes.

He watched Peter, hard at work in the garden, shearing, shaping all manner of shrubs, his tough hands never flinching from the wild growth. Manesty thought he might have missed his calling as a gardener, but in the same way a strong singer thinks he might be suited for the stage, or a natural athlete for the cricket field—pipe dreams, nothing more.

Peter's head snapped up as the gate opened and a ragged man stepped into his domain. Manesty thought the man looked in need of a good meal, so slim was he, his jacket and breeches hanging in sad folds from his frame. He walked toward Peter with a sailor's gait, offering his hand with a soft greeting. Manesty sat up straighter. Was it. . . ? Could it be. . . ?

He pushed back from the desk and raced around to the open door. His heart lurched in his chest as his eyes roamed the man's face—long, angular, and so much like his father's. Manesty felt tears spring to his eyes.

The lost son had found his way home.

"John!" Manesty tried to shout, but it came out as a croak through his tight throat.

The man looked up, a slow smile spreading across his tanned face. He crossed the plot in long strides, his hand already out before he reached the porch.

But Manesty ignored the hand, enfolding the man in a long, tight embrace, feeling his bones through the rough material. Then he pushed the man away, holding him at arm's length.

"Gother—" Manesty shook his head in frustration. "Your father—"

"I begged them not to tell you."

"But he's gone! Your father sails from the Nore even as we speak."

"I know. We exchanged letters." Newton sighed. "I had

hoped . . ." His voice trailed off, and he frowned down at his shoes.

Manesty leaned forward. "He would have liked you with him."

Newton nodded.

Manesty squeezed his shoulders. "Tea?"

He nodded again, and they stepped into the office, Newton folding himself into a chair as Manesty rang for the housekeeper. It was all bustle and exclamations before the tea table was set and the men relaxed, Manesty sipping and Newton sampling everything on the laden tray.

"Did Gother's cat survive the crossing?"

Newton shook his head as he spread clotted cream onto a biscuit. "If he had, we'd have eaten him."

It was quietly stated, with no humor, and Manesty blanched. Gother's report had been spare, barely mentioning their hardships. But he knew the extent of the *Greyhound*'s repairs, and he saw before him the condition of her passenger. He determined he would draw the entire tale out of the captain by week's end.

Newton ate with single-minded purpose, and Manesty took the opportunity to study him. The man was worn thin, his cheekbones pushing hard against hallowed skin. But he sat with an odd combination of confidence and humility, his shoulders back, his head down. There was tenderness in his bearing and warmth in his eyes. This was not the errant, arrogant son of yore. This was a man transformed.

Manesty itched to hear the genesis of the change but knew he'd have to bide his time until all would be revealed. He watched Newton stir sugar and cream into his cup and broached a less-treacherous subject.

"How are you on funds?"

Newton grimaced. "Very poor. Gother's news of a possible inheritance was, as I suspected, a ruse."

Manesty managed a concerned nod as he smiled inwardly. He'd have to congratulate the captain on his ingenuity. He leaned forward, circling his hands around his teacup.

"Do you have prospects for employment?"

"None."

"Excellent!" Manesty smiled. "I would like to offer you the *Brownlow*."

Newton's cup rattled on the saucer as he gently placed it on the table.

"She's a slaver, bound for Africa and South Carolina."

Manesty watched Newton struggle with the idea of going back to sea and sweetened the bid. "I offer you the captaincy."

Newton shook his head no, leaping out of his chair to stand at the window, his back to his benefactor.

Manesty cocked his head, frowning at the man as he murmured at the window. "John. . . ?"

Newton turned, a pensive look still on his features. "Virgil— 'He follows his father with unequal steps.' "

Manesty nodded thoughtfully, saying nothing, letting the son work out his troubles.

Newton inched back into the room, resting his hands on the back of his chair. "I cannot take the captaincy. But I will sail on the *Brownlow* as first mate, learn to submit to authority . . . learn to obey, before I demand it of others." And he smiled a sheepish, boyish smile.

Manesty was surprised at that admission, but readily agreed.

Newton returned to his seat and his tea, sipping in the comfortable silence until he looked up, his blue eyes showing a bit of panic. "When does she sail?"

"The latter part of July, I should hope."

"Well, then"—he set down his cup—"I must away to Kent, to see Miss Catlett."

Manesty's cup rattled this time, and he set it aside, clearing his throat, attempting to keep his voice even. "How long since you last saw her?"

"Three years."

"That is a lengthy separation."

Newton nodded, then the panicked look returned. "Has she—Do you know—" He nearly gasped the question. "Is she still . . . free?"

"I cannot say." And it was the truth. Manesty had given John's letters to Captain Ward and left it to that man's prudence to discard them or pass them on to the rightful recipient.

And now he found himself at odds with what was, what had been, and what should be. It was not in his nature to meddle in affairs of the heart. But he thought of Lord Clarendon, of his fine character and everything he had to offer a young woman. Had he offered himself yet? And Miss Catlett—had the letters destroyed any remnant of hope? Had she finally looked, really looked, at Clarendon—a man so perfectly suited to her? And if the two were now so engaged, what havoc would the arrival of the lost sailor play with their hearts?

"I have . . . survived . . . on slender faith. I pray, constantly pray . . ." Newton swallowed hard and spoke in a near whisper. "I know not how to live without the hope of her."

Manesty felt the ache in that bald statement, felt the quiet desperation. And so he posed his question with true compassion. "And if you arrive in Chatham and find that Miss Catlett has accepted another . . . What will you do, John?"

The man looked at him with such agony, Manesty almost regretted the question. Almost.

"I will take the *Brownlow* to Africa and then the colonies." His voice was resolute, if not steady. "But I will not come home. I will never come home."

Manesty looked at his friend's son so recently found, thought of the potential heartache awaiting him in Kent, and wondered, deep in his soul, if either of them could survive losing their boy again.

# CHAPTER

## 24

Chatham, Kent
Early June 1748

Mary glared at her brother's retreating back. How *dare* Jack call her a heartless, silly girl. She might not have his fine education, but she was still two years his elder. And he would do well to remember that.

She tried to hang on to her resentment, but the moment passed, and her shoulders slumped again in weary discontent. She laid her head against the arched window well and inhaled the wisteria's sweet fragrance as the purple blooms dangled just out of reach on the parlor's outside wall. The flowers danced in the warm breeze, taunting her with their abandon, in complete contrast to society's heavy constraints . . . on this side of the window.

For the first time in her life Mary wished her family would

go away. Every one of them had an opinion about her future and had no qualms about expressing it in myriad ways. Her father, no spendthrift in the past, liked to list the items one could purchase with a single guinea. And with unlimited guineas . . . why, the options were endless. Her mother was particularly inventive, never missing an opportunity to point out what a "lady" would do in this situation or that. But it was Jack who hounded her with speeches of duty and loyalty. And his vehemence left her stunned and troubled.

Not one of them considered *her* wishes—that it was *her* life, *her* "ever after" with which they fantasized and schemed. They seemed oblivious to her restlessness, indifferent to her confusion as she wandered from room to room, wondering if she would always be haunted by what might have been.

She heard the soft *tink* of rattling glass and turned to find young George dipping into their mother's prized candy dish, the delicate lid placed too close to the table's edge, as usual.

"George . . ." Mary warned and nearly laughed at his startled expression, the candy gripped in a pudgy hand.

"You'll not tell Mum," he pleaded, his eyes wide in the cherubic face.

She raised noncommittal eyebrows as she stepped from behind the chaise lounge, realizing as she moved that the myrtle linen of her summer dress all but matched the parlor's drapes. *A good hiding place,* she thought as she retrieved the lid and placed it over the hard bits of candy.

Her little brother retained his beseeching look even as he stuffed the sweetie into his mouth. She sank to his level, intending to review proper behavior, when the sound of boots in the hall drew their attention.

"Alex!" George launched himself against the man's legs, hugged him, then looked up with adoring eyes. "Did you bring Samson?"

"Not today, little man."

George snapped his fingers in dramatic disappointment. "Ods bodikins."

"George!" Mary scolded. Their mother would be horrified to hear the soft curse coming from her six-year-old's rosy lips.

"You'll not tell Mum," he pleaded again.

She opened her mouth, unwilling to let this transgression go but was interrupted by her mother's appearance in the door-frame. A conspiratorial look passed between brother and sister.

"Come along, George." His mother steered him down the hall with a hand atop his tawny head, and Alex grinned after them.

"Now, where do you suppose he's learning to swear?"

It was a rhetorical question. They both knew a dockyard town full of sailors and soldiers was a hotbed for coarse language. George would have a string of profanity at his disposal by age seven.

Mary grimaced, shaking her head, then cocked it in surprise as Alex turned and closed the parlor door. He gestured to the chairs before the fireplace, and they settled there, each of them perched on the edge of the cushion, their knees almost touching.

Alex smiled. "I'm in a bit of a pickle and hope you might . . . help me."

Mary's brow shot up, and she smiled in encouragement.

Alex plowed ahead. "The *Somerset* is practically finished, the Admiralty is ready to take command, and I have been offered a new commission."

Mary's heartbeat quickened. A new commission? Where? Why?

"The war is all but over, and a treaty's in the works, as your father has undoubtedly mentioned." He paused for Mary's nod. "The Admiralty would like to send me to the colonies."

She blinked. "C-colonies?"

He nodded and leaned forward, his green eyes glowing. "But, Mary," and his voice hushed with sincerity. "I will fight the commission—use the earl's influence, if I must—if you would do me the honor of becoming my wife."

And there it was—the moment Mary had anticipated since the Marine's warning . . . the moment she had played over and over in her mind as she searched her heart and prayed for direction. The moment that would force a choice.

The clock ticked on the mantel as his declaration hung between them. She took a steadying breath.

"Alex . . ." She made herself look straight into his eyes. "You are so truly . . . generous . . . in your admiration." She swallowed painfully. "But I cannot, in good conscience, commit myself to you."

His face still held that tender and hopeful expression, and she plunged ahead.

"My heart . . ." She felt her hand voluntarily move to the spot that ached so commonly now in her chest. "I gave my heart to another man, years ago, when we were just children. And even though he's . . . gone . . ." Her voice broke on that word, and the rest came out on a whisper. "I never really got it back."

She watched the light fade from his eyes, and her own filled with tears for the pain she knew she was causing him. God forgive her . . . "I'm so sorry. I—"

"I know." He reached for her hand, nodding. "I know. You long for John Newton." He tried to smile, and failed. "As I long for you."

The tears streamed down her cheeks as she gazed into his beautiful, tragic face. He was the best friend she'd ever had—a veritable match in personality. And now, a rebuffed opportunity.

He pulled a handkerchief from his breast pocket and pressed it into her hand, waiting as she dried her face and began to breathe a little easier.

"Well. 'The course of true love never did run smooth.'"

She smiled a little. *"A Midsummer Night's Dream."*

"Lysander to Hermia."

He stood then, looking down at her, several expressions crossing his face before he walked to the door. With his hand on the knob, he turned.

"May I write to you?"

"Yes. Of course."

He gave her another long, searching look, opened his mouth to speak, changed his mind, and walked through the door.

And deep within her soul, Mary felt with absolute clarity that Alexander Todd, reluctant viscount, decorated Navy captain, and loyal companion, had just walked out of her life. Forever.

---

*Late June*

Mary huddled in her window seat, staring blindly at the harbor, her heart thudding in heavy tempo. Two weeks had passed since Alex's proposal. He had quit Chatham the very next day, sailing with his regiment to London and then to the colonies.

Neither of them had spoken to others about their last conversation. But her family—even the Marine—seemed to accuse her of driving Alex away. Many angry words and cold glances came her direction, and she received all of them in silence. She simply could not muster the energy to fight.

*"Hope deferred maketh the heart sick,"* the widow had quoted as she'd sat by her own attic window, waiting, working through her own yearning and sadness. Hope deferred. Mary had made her decision—she had chosen to trust in God, to wait, to pray for John Newton.

But was her hope blinding her judgment? Was she being faithful or merely stubborn?

*But when the desire cometh* . . . the Proverb continued. Mary shook her head. She would not dwell on wishes any more today.

The London stage caught her eye as it pulled up to the coach office on High Street. It was running several hours late, and the waiting passengers were in a dither. She smiled a little as she watched the driver prod them back with the end of his whip. He muscled his way to the coach's side, lowered the steps, and opened the door.

Out popped an overdressed matron, fanning her florid face with a limp handkerchief. The driver handed her down, and the crowd backed away at her haughty stare. A maid followed, then a well-dressed man, and then a sailor who turned immediately right, pushing his way through the—

Mary sat ramrod straight, her jaw slack, astonishment tingling across her pale skin. She knew that tall frame—the squared shoulders, the sharp features, the auburn hair.

She stared only a moment longer, then tore down the stairs, her heart beating wildly. The months, the years of waiting and wondering seemed trivial now. For just as her heart had whispered and the widow had believed—just as God had planned, the lost sailor had come home. John Newton had come home.

# CHAPTER

## ❧ 25 ❧

*Olney Parish, Buckinghamshire*
*December 31, 1772*

T he vicar opened his eyes to the dying fire and smiled. After nearly a quarter century, he still remembered the tiniest details of the day he walked into the Catlett home, five years after his first visit—a ghost returned from the sea.

He remembered Jack's astonishment, then joy, as the boy— tall and not quite a man—pounded his bony back, shouting for all to come, come see who's here! Mrs. Catlett expressed no less surprise before frowning at his thinness, telling him to just come to the kitchen and she would fatten him up. But it was Mary, standing mute in the hall, who kept him rooted to the spot.

She was so lovely—a woman at last, her ginger hair loose around her shoulders, her rosy mouth shaped into a startled O. She'd worn a dress the color of summer hydrangeas that matched her blue eyes, wide against ashen skin. He'd stared at her in awkward silence until a blush crept up her neck and she spun on her heel, leaving him in the hall with her laughing brother.

It was not until evening that he found her in the back parlor, resting on the floral chaise. He sat at her side and took her hand, and his heart was so full he found he could not form a sentence. He was much more eloquent with a pen and a sheaf of paper.

It was years later, after their marriage, after a fit of apoplexy grounded him from the sea and he'd accepted the post of customs officer, that Newton discovered how close he'd come to losing her. His heart ached for her even now, remembering the morning he'd casually glanced through the newspaper, remarking that the earl of Clarendon had died without an heir . . . how her spoon had clattered to the floor and her face had drained of color. She would not speak of it—of the loss of her great friend, the reluctant viscount. Jack had filled in the details of the man's demise in the Seven Years' War.

But it was then that he began to think in "ifs." If he had never gone to sea, never been enslaved, never suffered through that terrible storm . . . If his father, Manesty, Gother had left him to his own designs on the Ivory Coast . . . If any of the events of his life, great or small, had fallen out of place, if God's design had failed, all . . . all would be lost to him.

It was an exercise he repeated often. It was why he kept the diaries—to remind him that the Lord had wrought a marvelous thing. That he had been, but was no longer, an infidel.

But oh . . . the depth of his degeneracy recorded and alluded to in those pages. He ran his hand over the worn leather cover stamped "1751"—the year of his first captaincy, the year after his father drowned at Fort York, the year he decided to start recording the events of his life . . . truthfully, boldly. He did not have to open the book to remember. He could see his hand inscribing the first page, writing in the bold script of a twenty-five-year-old opportunist: *It will be pleasant to remember these things afterwards.*

But it had not been pleasant. He'd opened the book for the first and last time eight years ago as he was preparing a narrative that became his autobiography. Perhaps it was maturity. Perhaps it was his burgeoning friendship with the preacher John Wesley. Whatever the cause, he'd read the details recorded there with disgust and shame. Even as a captain he'd found the slave trade with its chains and bolts and shackles repugnant, but not for the honorable reasons Wesley and the Quakers claimed—not for its *moral* depravity. And as his autobiography garnered attention and the abolitionist movement gained momentum, there were personal calls for access to the four-year detailed accounts of his three voyages as slave-ship captain.

He sighed and stood to stoke the fire, the diary placed far from the hungry flames. No matter his humiliation, he could not dispose of these records whilst they still might be of use. The Lord would not let him.

He carried the book to his desk, noting that snow still fell in profusion outside the attic room. The chair creaked as he settled in and placed the worn book in the drawer's secret compartment with the others.

He turned his attention to another, larger, leather-bound book open on his desk—a catalogue of seventeen years' musings, 1755 to today. He had a final entry to make. He sat with pen poised over paper, but his mind remained with the past.

He turned to a page from 1766 and read: *I am a poor wretch that once wandered naked and barefoot, without a home, without a friend . . .* He turned again and found a scriptural note on John 9:25: *One thing I know, that, whereas I was blind, now I see.* Now I see . . . On many pages the words *mercy* and *grace* leapt out at him, and he considered that whilst the tenets of mercy had been clear to him from the moment he received it in the London-derry nave, the significance of grace had dawned slowly.

Grace, he learned, could not be earned. One could not demand it. It could not be bartered or purchased or filched. Grace was a gift—a gift no one deserved. And it was, without doubt, the most wonderful discovery of his life. He thought Robert Robinson had defined it so perfectly in his hymn, "Come Thou Fount": *O to grace how great a debtor daily I'm constrained to be!*

Newton looked to his own hymn on grace, a work in prog-ress for the New Year's Day service. He pulled the sheet of paper toward him, his practiced eye running over the rhyme and rhythm. The last three stanzas had come quickly and remained unedited. But the muse still stumbled over the first three.

He turned again to the diary, scribbling words and phrases on the hymn sheet as they appealed to him. He shook his head as he read. The start of 1764 had not been good, as he and Mary had agonized over the decision to leave his lucrative customs job for the ministry. To serve the Church of England as priest was a dream he'd finally found within his grasp. But it assured a life of genteel poverty, and the Catletts had revolted at the idea. Their ridicule still stung. And then, the same year, the awful shock of Jack's

death . . . the laughter silenced after just thirty-three years. Newton touched the spots where his tears had dropped upon the paper.

So many hardships, so many uncertainties . . . all resolved in
time through God's benevolence. And now here he was—vicar
of Olney Parish . . . an African blasphemer transformed by
grace. He smiled and began to write.

Hours later he again took his place in the great leather chair
before the hearth, relit his Alderman, and read the lines he
would read to his congregants on the morrow:

*Amazing grace! how sweet the sound*
*That saved a wretch like me!*
*I once was lost, but now am found,*
*Was blind, but now I see.*

*'Twas grace that taught my heart to fear.*
*And grace my fears reliev'd;*
*How precious did that grace appear*
*The hour I first believ'd!*

*Thro' many dangers, toils and snares,*
*I have already come;*
*'Tis grace hath brought me safe thus far,*
*And grace will lead me home.*

*The Lord has promis'd good to me,*
*His word my hope secures;*
*He will my shield and portion be,*
*As long as life endures.*

*Yes, when this flesh and heart shall fail,*
*And mortal life shall cease,*

*I shall possess, within the veil,*
*A life of joy and peace.*

*The earth shall soon dissolve like snow,*
*The sun forbear to shine;*
*But God, Who call'd me here below,*
*Will be forever mine.*

Newton laid the page on his lap and stared into the fire. He was forty-seven years old and still amazed by grace.

A knock sounded at his door, and he looked up to find Mary bustling in with tea. He watched her arrange the items just so, smiling and humming a Christmas melody. His heart still trembled with a powerful love for her, still left him mute at times. But the longing that had gripped him twenty-five years ago—the restlessness, the sorrow—had been swept away.

Theirs was a remarkable story—an innocent, tender love story novelists tried so hard to invent on the page. Cynics did not understand their devotion, how their bond, forged in childhood and tested in the silent battle of time and distance, only strengthened by the day . . . by the hour. They had but one heart between them.

Mary rounded the desk and handed him a cup of steaming tea, peering over his shoulder at the hymn on his lap. He leaned back his head and watched her face as she read. She was so much more to him than a wife. She had saved him, time and again, from himself.

She was a gift. She was grace . . . the sweet, sweet sound of grace.

# EPILOGUE

No one—least of all, John Newton—knew what an impact "Amazing Grace" would eventually have upon the world. It was just another weekly hymn, transcribed and read to a roomful of congregants New Year's Day, 1773, then put away until it was included in a 1779 collection of *Olney Hymns*. William Cowper, Newton's friend and unpublished poet, contributed to the hymnbook that had an initial printing of one thousand copies. The Church of England rejected it as "unscriptural, schismatic, and doctrinally dangerous." But Newton's influence could not be stopped.

The *Authentic Narrative* of his life—more thriller than strict autobiography—coupled with multiple *Hymns* reprints and a move to St. Mary Woolnoth Church in London launched him into social prominence. The "slave-ship captain turned priest" appealed to the hearts and minds of society, and every manner of person—from the illiterate to the elite—sought out the African blasphemer for comfort and advice.

The diaries that proved such a transformation stayed locked away until the mid–1780s when William Wilberforce, a Tory and abolitionist, knocked on Newton's parish door. Although

Newton had long abhorred the slave trade, his public commitment to abolishing it began with that single knock. With the diaries' details before him, Newton composed a ten-thousand-word rousing confession and professional report entitled "Thoughts Upon the African Slave Trade." On the title page he quoted Matthew 7:12, Jesus' words during the Sermon on the Mount—"Therefore all things whatsoever ye would that men should do to you, do ye even so to them: for this is the law and the prophets." We call it the Golden Rule. Newton thought it the foundation of goodness and mercy due every human.

Soon after its publication, Newton spoke before the House of Commons, his diaries, letters, essay, autobiography, and first-hand knowledge powerful weapons against a Parliament determined to endorse slavery as an economic necessity. But even as Newton helped the abolitionists gain ground politically, he was losing a personal battle at home.

In her bed by the window, Mary lay dying from breast cancer. Her illness was nearly his undoing. After forty years of marriage, and what he considered one of the great love stories of all time, Newton struggled to let her go. But he did, December 15, 1790. She was sixty-one years old. For months afterward he wandered from room to room, quoting lines from a Cowper poem . . . "I carry the arrow with me wherever I go. I cannot forget her—no! not for five minutes."

Tucked away in Mary's private possessions was a cache of love letters he'd sent her during his four voyages to Africa. Three years after her death, Newton compiled these into two volumes and published *Letters to a Wife*—a memorial to his beloved and a testimony to happy wedded life.

And the battle for slavery raged on.

Newton used his ever-growing reputation for the abolition movement, partnering with Wilberforce, Cowper, and activist Hannah More, to appeal to social conscience. In 1807, after a twenty-year crusade and eleven defeats, Parliament passed the Abolition of the Slave Trade Act. George III assented and the British slave trade was finally illegal. Another fifty-eight years passed before the United States adopted the Thirteenth Amendment and abolished slavery in America.

On December 21, 1807, nine months after the Parliamentary victory, the elderly Newton died in London. He was eighty-two. Although buried together beneath the St. Mary Woolnoth sanctuary, the Newtons' remains were removed to the Olney graveyard in 1873.

Newton never witnessed the extraordinary popularity of his hymn "Amazing Grace." Indeed, hymnologists did not consider this hymn extraordinary at all, choosing Newton's "Glorious Things of Thee Are Spoken" and "How Sweet the Name of Jesus Sounds" as better representations of his hymn-writing skills.

After dozens of different tunes accompanied Newton's verse, the now-famous melody, "New Britain," was adopted in 1835 and published in *Southern Harmony*. It is widely considered an old American plantation song, pentatonic—using only five different tones—and rife with slavery inferences.

In 1910 an anonymous source wrote the stanza:

*When we've been there ten thousand years,*
*Bright shining as the sun,*

*We've no less days to sing God's praise*
*Than when we first begun.*

This verse first appeared in Edwin Othello Excell's *Coronation Hymns* as a substitute for Newton's original last stanzas and remains with his verse today.

The hymn gained momentum during the Civil War, but it was Mahalia Jackson's rendition during World War II, Martin Luther King Jr.'s civil rights marches of the 1960s, and the 1972 bagpipe version of the Royal Scots Dragoon Guards that launched it into worldwide fame.

Newton's final diary entry was on the fifty-seventh anniversary of the pivotal storm in the North Atlantic. He never forgot his cry for help and the Lord's answer. He never forgot he'd been saved by grace.

Fittingly, he had the last word on his long and influential life by writing his own epitaph. Inscribed in marble and resting beside the St. Mary Woolnoth pulpit, it reads:

JOHN NEWTON
CLERK
ONCE AN INFIDEL AND LIBERTINE,
A SERVANT OF SLAVES IN AFRICA,
WAS
BY THE RICH MERCY OF OUR LORD AND SAVIOUR
JESUS CHRIST,
PRESERVED, RESTORED, PARDONED,
AND APPOINTED TO PREACH THE FAITH
HE HAD LONG LABORED TO DESTROY.

# THANKS TO:

M y loyal early draft readers: Pam Clanton, Cory Ridenhour, and Sondra Schaub. I always tell them, "Be brutal!" And they are . . . wonderfully so.

Gary Wollenhaupt for his ever-patient guy-in-the-basement researching skills. Nothing throws him. Nothing.

Corey Schaub for his expert advice on eighteenth-century weaponry. Who knew my main character would have to have two left hands to cock two pistols simultaneously? Corey did . . . and I avoided a reader's grimace and eye roll in the process.

Betsy Yarborough for accompanying me to Europe to research this book. Oh, the memories, the subways, the crêpes . . .

The staff at the British Library in London and Chatham Library in Kent who patiently answered this fast-talking Yankee's many, many questions.

And enormous gratitude to those who've already documented so much of John Newton's life, including: Richard Cecil in *The Life of John Newton*, William E. Phipps in *Amazing Grace in John Newton*, and John Newton himself in *An Authentic Narrative*. But I especially want to thank Steve Turner for not only his wonderfully researched and written *Amazing Grace*—what I consider the best available biography of the man and song—but also for his ongoing guidance while I struggled through the details of a life and hymn lived two centuries past.

—*CAS*

July 2006

CHRISTINE SCHAUB is an accomplished writer, speaker, actor, and pianist. *Finding Anna,* her debut novel, launched the MUSIC OF THE HEART series and received instant acclaim from reviewers. Schaub lives in Nashville, Tennessee, and invites readers to contact her at thelongingseason@aol.com.

# 235 *Amazing Grace*

JOHN NEWTON

E. O. E. Arr.

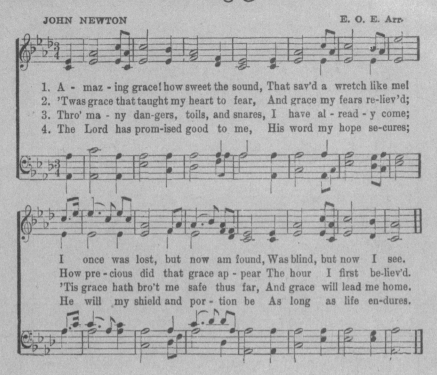

1. A - maz - ing grace! how sweet the sound, That sav'd a wretch like me!
2. 'Twas grace that taught my heart to fear, And grace my fears re-liev'd;
3. Thro' ma - ny dan-gers, toils, and snares, I have al - read - y come;
4. The Lord has prom-ised good to me, His word my hope se-cures;

I once was lost, but now am found, Was blind, but now I see.
How pre - cious did that grace ap - pear The hour I first be-liev'd.
'Tis grace hath bro't me safe thus far, And grace will lead me home.
He will my shield and por - tion be As long as life en-dures.

EXCERPT FROM *Finding Anna*
BY CHRISTINE SCHAUB

*Chicago*
*Sunday, October 8, 1871*

S pafford stood with a thousand other spectators on the east
bank of the Chicago River and simply stared. What he saw
was breathtaking in its awful beauty.

For half a mile real estate on the west side of the river glowed
orange. Flames danced across the night sky, reflecting off the
water, bathing everyone and everything on the riverbank in the
warmth of firelight. A wind blew, carrying across the fire's
*crackle-pop* and smell of burning pine. It had all the elements of
an early winter evening beside the hearth.

The night was full of sound as steam pumpers clattered down
the street, horses' hooves pounding over the Madison Street
Bridge, fire marshals and engine foremen shouting orders
through their brass-speaking trumpets. The crowd reacted with
"oohs" and "ahhs" when the first spray of water doused the
burning wood and sent up great clouds of steam, as if from a
giant teakettle. The observers pointed and exclaimed, specula-

tion passing in and out of the crowd. "That Irishman, Patrick O'Leary . . ." ". . . firemen into the whiskey . . ." ". . . flames out of control . . ."

And because no one had Tuesday's hindsight, because the madness and weeping had not even begun, because no one had the premonition of disaster, the mood was light and festive.

On this side of the river.

A gust of wind suddenly rushed through the crowd, sending hats and hairpins flying and coattails flapping. Spafford made an expert catch of his own hat as it lifted off his head and settled it precisely back into place.

Everything about the man was precise. He stood exactly six feet with a stalwart frame toned by a preference for walking the rambling route between his law office, the business district, and his vast real estate holdings. His features were strictly patrician and set at perfect angles—the square jaw and sculpted lips, the linear Roman nose, the spike-lashed eyes below arched brows.

He had even aged with perfection. His coal black hair showed gray only at the temples, and tiny lines fanned out from intelligent black eyes set in a perpetually tanned complexion.

He was as meticulous about his appearance as he was his business dealings. His suits were pressed, boots shined, nails trimmed, beard clean-shaven. His stance was both erect and skillfully passive, with no telltale signs of his state of mind.

His precision created an air of excellence and wisdom that inspired men to treat him with respect. His clients and business partners considered him a fair man, and he appreciated that. They also were a bit afraid of the furrowed brow, stubborn jaw, and piercing stare when he was displeased. And that suited him.

At the moment, his lips pursed in silent concern. While the crowd pointed and bantered with no sign of disbursing at such a late hour, the fire seemed to grow. It looked to him to be every bit as big as last night's blaze that had destroyed five square blocks and required sixteen hours of diligent fire fighting.

He squinted at his watch in the glow of the firelight—close to midnight. Nearly an hour and a half had passed since he'd stepped outside the Opera House and followed the crowd to the riverbank. He really should go home. He stole a last glance across the water, then watched in morbid fascination as the unthinkable happened.

The fire jumped the river.

In one dreadful moment, the wood on the great steeple of St. Paul's Church ignited, caught the wind, and rode to the east side in a terrific shower of sparks. The crowd gasped almost in unison, and shouts of "Across the river!" followed. Within minutes smoke began to choke the bystanders, and they backed en masse up Market Street and across Madison into the heart of downtown Chicago.

Spafford moved with the crowd and, like most of the hurrying people, kept turning to look behind him, surprised at the rolling clouds of smoke and ash caught up in the wind and moving ever faster with them. The night sky was lit with a strange dancing light that cast the familiar into curious shapes and angles. Almost without notice he was in the midst of a block of brick buildings, tall and serene and wholly unfamiliar. He turned about several times, searching for a landmark, and spied a statue of George Washington atop a fierce pawing stallion of the richest black. The president sat the saddle with complete confidence, shoulders back, pointing the way.

*Ah, Washington Street,* he mused and headed in that direction.

The whole commercial center was electric with hotel guests, businessmen, and late-night sightseers milling about the courthouse lawns, conversing over the clanging of the massive bell that signaled *fire*. The weeks of fall had been unspectacular in their dryness. The leaves did not change color as much as shrivel up like old paper bags, then hang dejectedly until a stale wind coaxed them to the ground to scuttle along the wooden streets. By October the drought-ridden city was averaging six fires a day, and a good blaze on a warm Sunday night kept the crowd outside and buzzing with excitement.

He stood gazing hypnotically at the colorful sky until it occurred to him that if he could catch a bridge across the river, he could watch the fire's progress from a safe distance and height . . . in his own office.

He turned up Clark Street and arrived at the river just in time to watch the iron swing bridge, loaded with people, halt in the middle of the river while ships of every size passed through to Lake Michigan—a curious sight for the middle of the night. He'd had the misfortune of being "bridged" for long stretches of time and considered the LaSalle Street Tunnel a better option.

Off he headed down Clark, turning west on Lake Street. At the corner he looked toward the Sherman House and was surprised to see that during his short trek the formerly passive crowd had turned anxious. The sidewalks were crammed full of people looking upward, shielding their eyes against the falling ash. Guests hung out of hotel windows, pointing and shouting, their words tossed into the wind. Spafford listened closely but could decipher nothing until it was passed down the street toward him. And then what he heard made his blood run cold.

The gasworks were on fire.

The explosions started soon after, and the already anxious crowd panicked. Spafford raced down the next block and turned on LaSalle. The tunnel—just opened in July—loomed ahead. The vehicles in the center passageways were moving in a calm and orderly fashion, both north and south, and the footway glowed under the lights, revealing pedestrians moving steadily.

Spafford stepped into the underground highway and walked quickly under the river. The air was moist and cool here, and he relaxed for the first time in an hour. He started devising a plan. He would go to his office, secure essential documents, then look for a cab that would take him north into Lake View. The hour must be excessively late. He reached for his pocket watch, trying to guess at the time when, without so much as a flicker, the gaslights went out. A moment of stunned silence was followed by the screams of horse and driver plunged into total blackness. *Fool!* He admonished himself. *You knew the gasworks were in flames.* Through the stone wall Spafford heard the unmistakable sounds of a mass of frightened humanity trapped underground with skittish horses.

People in the footway had come to an immediate halt. Seconds ticked by, then a murmuring began, followed by a slow jostling, then apologies all around as strangers collided in the darkness. And then, gridlock. Their side of the tunnel was remarkably quiet and composed while they waited for verbal direction passed down from either end. People stood amicably, breathing in and out. The scent of lavender drifted toward him, and he thought of his wife, abed several hours by now.

He pictured her there. Her golden hair would be tied with a ribbon to match the trim of her nightgown. She would be lying on her side, one hand tucked under her cheek, a child's pose that suited her delicate features. When he slid into bed, she would open her eyes and smile ever so briefly, revealing very white and even teeth. And then she would return to her slumber on the lavender-scented sheets, content that he was beside her.

*Content* was a word he used often with Anna. Her Norwegian heritage had instilled in her a realism and discipline that resulted in few surprises. She was neither dramatic nor excessive, like so many wives of his colleagues, and therefore rarely dissatisfied. She'd had certain simple expectations when she'd married him—a cheerful home filled with flowers and children, a dining room open to friends and strangers alike for long lively suppers, a parlor for entertainment round the piano.

And that's what he had given her. His business success had allowed him to give her more, but she'd never come to expect it. And her surprise and delight at each gift, at each thoughtful gesture, was Elysium to him.

A more intense jostling brought him back to the tunnel, and the word was passed: North. All pedestrians must travel north. There was an edge of urgency to the message, and Spafford wondered at it as the crowd shuffled along in the darkness, then gained a little space, then moved freely under the river.

At last he was out of the tunnel and onto the ramp, then on the wooden sidewalk, clattering along with the crowd now laughing with embarrassment and relief. And then in slow motion, it seemed, they all turned and looked behind them.

Across the Chicago River, as close as Washington Street, the business district was consumed with red tongues of light. It seemed impossible, as he had just come from there. He stared in wonder. The Chamber of Commerce, Brunswick Hall, and Methodist Church all seemed to be burning. That would have to mean Farwell Hall was destroyed, and the Reynolds Block and McVicker's Theatre. It looked to be a wall of flame for blocks behind those buildings. His spirit took a tremendous plunge.

He was ruined.

All the money he and his friends had invested just this spring in land—land to the north, land in the direction of an expanding city—was folly. Chicago would not expand. It might not even recover. His ears were ringing with alarm, and he shook his head to clear them.

The fire brigade pulled up and began pumping the chilly water directly from the river and throwing it onto the facing buildings. "Little Giant" was stamped across the engine's side, and indeed, it looked to be a David and Goliath moment. Spafford turned up LaSalle and prayed they could stop this violence.

Within moments he was standing outside his office building, torn between continuing on to Anna or gathering essential paperwork from his desk and safe.

Somewhere a bell tolled one.

Spafford looked up. The unmistakable glow of kerosene lamps lit the upper-floor windows with a soft, inviting light. He hung his head. McDaid was inside and must be told of their loss.

He dragged himself up the stairs, forming the words that

would forever change his partner's life and livelihood. At the landing he scanned the brass nameplate:

SPAFFORD & McDAID
ESTABLISHED 1867

Five years they'd worked together, two with another partner, the last three comfortably paired in Rooms 4 and 5 at 147 La-Salle.

The office was open, and Spafford stood in the doorway watching his partner sort methodically through a mound of papers. He stepped into the room and clicked the door shut. McDaid looked up from the files just long enough to acknowledge him.

"The real estate paperwork is scattered. Truly, I thought it more organized."

Spafford grimaced. "Leave it."

McDaid ignored him. "I've managed to find the original investment with all signatures and the profit forecast—"

"Henry."

McDaid looked up, a wariness in his eyes.

"The business district is gone."

"Gone?"

"I stood at the river and watched it burn. The hotels, the banks, the theatres—all are gone."

Several emotions flashed across McDaid's face—confusion, disbelief, horror, and finally resignation. Spafford knew the same realization had struck his partner—that the bulk of their investment, land for enlarging parks and expanding a growing metropolis, was useless now. For who could think of such trivialities when an entire commercial city must be rebuilt? He noted how his partner's shoulders slumped, then squared as he carefully organized the paperwork and slid it into his valise anyway.

Spafford watched him work a few more moments. Theirs was an easy partnership. Where he was outspoken—even blunt—with clients, McDaid was reserved and cautious. His partner could sit through hours of meetings, taking meticulous notes, smiling at the animated bantering, and speak no more than five words. While he itched to be out, surveying new properties and soliciting clients, his partner was content to work complex financial equations and pore over tedious real estate law at his desk. Their personalities and skills were a true complement to each other. It was what made the law firm of Spafford & McDaid so successful.

But their partnership was more than that. McDaid was deceptively smart, driven, and a gentleman—in short, the brother Spafford had always wanted. He had never known a kinder, gentler man than Henry McDaid—a man no one hated, a man who would drop his jaw in astonishment to learn that his partner aspired to be more like him.

A gale-like wind shook the building, rattling the windows, and the men looked up and out in unison. Beyond the panes it looked as if a snowstorm was in full force . . . little flakes of ash stained with fire.

Spafford's hands hung at his sides like iron weights. The futility of it all overwhelmed him. He could not even bring himself to step into the adjoining law library with its leather-bound volumes of books—books on which he'd lavished so much money and pride. But McDaid's persistent sorting and storing provided a purpose and a glimmer of hope that they would recover from this, that all would not be lost. He moved to his desk and started to work.

No words passed between the two men as they saved and discarded papers pertinent to their corporate survival. Land leases, client histories, court judgments came and went.

When the glass on the windows facing the street cracked and the frames began to smoke, they worked faster. When their valises bulged, they removed large documents to the steel safe and became more selective.

When smoke crept into the room and hovered near the ceiling, Spafford consulted his watch—half past two. He moved to the window and peered out through the rolling fumes. In the distance, aglow like a warrior's torch, the courthouse's grand cupola blazed in majestic beauty. As he watched, the tower glowed even brighter, then crumbled inward, the massive bell still clanging until, with a resounding thud that shook the earth, the symbol of a thousand civic ceremonies and celebrations tolled no more.

He was surprised at the tears that sprang to his eyes. He wanted to weep at the destruction before him and bowed his head, schooling his emotions until the intense heat emanating from the cracked glass forced him to jerk back.

He looked toward the street, and what he saw and heard in that brief moment was enough to propel him into action. He grabbed his valise off his desk, fastened it, and turned to McDaid.

"We must go. Now."

McDaid never slowed. "Just a few more documents."

Spafford stopped him with a viselike grip on his upper arm. "The sidewalks are on fire and people are stampeding in the street. We are in danger here."

As if in emphasis, a ball of flame burst through the window, scattering little pockets of fire across the room, igniting stacks of papers. McDaid slammed and locked the safe, then grabbed his valise, and the two men dashed out the door and down the stairs.

At street level, the scene was pure chaos. The door had burst open and flames from the sidewalk licked at the frame. In the street, panic-stricken people pushed and shoved, screaming children crushed behind their parents, and everywhere cinders fell like snowflakes, lighting new fires.

Spafford took one look and pushed McDaid back into the hallway. He was shouting now, the street noise and roar of collapsing buildings deafening. "You must get to Anna if I cannot. And I will do the same with Dora. Lake View may be too close to the forest to be spared. Go to the north beach in Lincoln Park. Anna knows the place. I will find her there."

McDaid nodded. "God be with you." The partners and friends clasped hands and locked eyes now red from smoke.

"And also with you."

Out the door they ran, leaping across the burning sidewalk and into the masses of stampeding people. It was futile to do anything but move with the crowd as it surged forward, the leaders searching for a street or alleyway not yet consumed by smoke and fire.

Barely one block west the crowd came to a bone-crushing halt, and Spafford turned his head, looked back, and watched as the law offices of Spafford & McDaid, against a backdrop of a lurid yellowish red, crumbled to the ground. The collapse made a tremendous roar and sent a storm cloud of dust and cinders rolling down the jammed street. And as he threw up his hand to shield his eyes, he instinctively thought of the biblical promise that in hell everyone will be salted with fire.

He clutched his valise to his chest and his hat to his head and determined he would not test that promise today.

He watched the destruction march toward him, masses of flames bounding from building to building, and could see that the pace of the fire would soon outmatch that of the crowd. He cast about for McDaid, not finding him, then fought his way to the street's edge and leapt onto the elevated sidewalk, jumping over flaming wood and bundles, halting at the edge of Wells.

Here, the route was swarming with a rush of people streaming across the Wells Street Bridge on horseback, in carts, carriages, wheelbarrows, and every type of conveyance. Horses pranced and tore at their harnesses. Stray cows, dogs, and cats ran terrified through the people on foot. The din of screaming children and animals and shouts of "North! North!" was terrible.

He calculated his odds and decided to continue westward toward the north branch of the river. It was no more than four blocks away, and he could fling himself into the water if the heat and fumes became too great. A plan formed as he fought his way across the crowd. He would get to the river and cross at the railroad trestle on Kinzie. The area was nothing but iron track. Surely it would not burn.

But he underestimated the desperation of the fleeing crowd. He tried to push westward, and the people dragged him north.

He watched a man on horseback force his way through, flinging a whip left and right, his horse trampling those who would not yield. He wanted to tear the brute from his saddle and watched in some satisfaction as many of those marked by the whip did just that.

And always they were just moments from being consumed by the fire.

They were surrounded now by near-constant explosions of stores of oil and other combustible material. Windows blew out, showering them with glass, tearing into their skin. Buildings fell with a force, their bricks, boards, and burning shingles picked up by a hurricane wind and flung over their heads, falling around them, setting their hair and clothing ablaze.

It was more horrific than any description of the bowels of hell.

At last, singed and bleeding, his hat still miraculously on his head, Spafford was on the other side and at an intersection he was sure was Wells and Ohio. He turned left and was suddenly, eerily, alone.

Buildings burned on both sides of the street, and the air was so full of dust that he could see no more than half a block ahead. He hesitated, glancing back at the mass of stampeding people. Should he go west when everyone else headed north? The wrong decision could cost him his life.

A sudden, terrific explosion pitched him forward and blew his waistcoat over his head. He tumbled like an oak leaf down the burning street, his valise clutched tightly against his chest, and slid to a halt against a stack of bricks.

His body numb and hearing muffled, he scooted to an

upright position and tried to disentangle his coat from his head. Hot, sticky objects slapped against him, and he ducked down, deciding to leave the coat in place and peer out at his surroundings.

Truly the Day of Judgment had come.

The air was full of firebrands—little red and yellow devils that darted and swirled through the street, tugging burning planks and shingles along like kites. He watched in disbelief as a marble-topped dresser danced silently by, collecting embers in its open drawers. A man's shirt sailed close behind, sleeve outstretched, waving good-bye.

He shook his head. He felt as if he were in a dream—a nightmare with no sound and no escape. Yet he was awake and alive and still in command of his limbs.

The ground rumbled and the wall at his back collapsed inward, sending up and out a cloud of dust so thick he could see no more than a few feet around him.

He struggled to his feet, peeking out through the coat, hearing little. A curtain of embers fell in front of him and lit the street. The gale-force winds still blew but now were filled with particles that pinged against his torso like sewing needles. He turned and followed the wind, the needles at his back.

———————

*Monday, October 9, 1871*

He woke with a yell and looked wildly about him. The children! Where were his children! He groped around for Bessie, reaching for her little arms still pudgy with baby fat. His hand connected with rough wood, and his surroundings came into slow focus.

He was on a pile of lumber, on a dock, on the edge of the river. It was daylight, but the sky was overcast and hazy with smoke, and as far as the eye could see north and south, across the river, Chicago was aflame. The Queen City of the West was no more. He stared at the sight, dry-eyed.

What time was it? He pulled his watch from his waistcoat, blinked down at it, then remembered. The crystal on his watch had shattered in the explosion, and the mechanism had stopped at three minutes after four o'clock this morning. He recalled fighting his way to the river, crossing at Kinzie Street, turning down Canal, and collapsing close to the water. He looked around and recognized his whereabouts as Avery's Lumberyard.

He lay back down, sick of the sight of burning buildings, sick of the running, desperate for a drink of cool water. He closed his eyes and immediately opened them as his nightmare returned. Anna was there, surrounded by Annie, Maggie, and Bessie, baby Tanetta in her arms. They were gathered in the parlor around the rosewood piano, holding quite still for a family photo. Except, he was not with them. He was standing in the hallway watching them smile, watching the picture start to burn around the edges, watching the flames move closer and closer, shouting at them to *run!* Watching in horror as they kept smiling, even while the flames licked at their faces.

Tears streamed down his cheeks, and he forced himself off the lumber pile with a sob. He had to keep moving. He had to find his family.

He turned north and followed the river, still clutching his

battered valise. He trudged block after block, choked by the smoke, his throat screaming for moisture. Not a soul was on the streets, and he supposed they had fled west to the prairies when word came that this fire jumped rivers. But it hadn't crossed the river here. Not yet.

He finally reached Chicago Avenue and found a well where, mercifully, someone had left a tin cup. He pumped the handle and fresh water trickled out, just enough for a desperate man and a little cup. The feel of it on his tongue and throat was enough to move him to tears again. He choked them down, rested no more than ten minutes, and continued north.

By nightfall he came to North Avenue. He had spent precious time at each street crossing, turning east to the edge of the water, turning back from the flames, then finding a way across the river's north branch, then back to the canal. As dusk settled, he realized he'd walked all day and covered less than two miles.

A current of defeat coursed through him. He would never make it in time. He would die failing to protect his family. He leaned against a wooden fence, slid down to the ground, and wept like a child. The burning photo played over and over in his mind. He tried to think. He tried to pray. But all that came to his mind were snippets of verses about hell, being cast into hell . . . soul and body in hell . . . the rich man in hell.

He tried to think of better verses. He would recite the Twenty-third Psalm. But how did it go? Panic was taking over his mind. He couldn't think. He couldn't breathe. He was sick with worry.

And then he heard a voice—not his own—from deep within.

*Pray.*

He was trying to pray, but he could not remember the psalm! It had always been such a comfort to him, and now he could not even recall—David! King David wrote it. He was sure of that. But he wasn't always a king. He was a . . . a . . .

*Speak to me . . . from your own heart.*

His mind went blank. From his *own* heart? He couldn't. He didn't know where to begin. What could he say that could possibly be more eloquent, more worthy, than the words of a king?

*Come to me . . .*

He heard the voice and instantly his heart completed the phrase. *And I will give you rest.*

So he sat perfectly still somewhere on North Avenue, just yards from fallen walls and blackened trees, and for the first time in his forty-three years, he bared his soul and had a simple conversation with the Lord.

# Looking for More Good Books to Read?